TWIN STARS

VOLUME 1 OF *THE GANNET QUARTET*

This book was donated
by Charlotte, and brought
here by her sisters—
volunteers
        Harriet
    Lucinda Victoria

This is an IndieMosh book

brought to you by MoshPit Publishing
an imprint of Mosher's Business Support Pty Ltd

PO Box 4363
Penrith Plaza NSW 2750

indiemosh.com.au

 A catalogue record for this
work is available from the
NATIONAL
LIBRARY National Library of Australia
OF AUSTRALIA

https://www.nla.gov.au/collections

Title: Twin Stars

Series: The Gannet Quartet; Volume 1

Author: Clutterbuck, Charlotte (1950–)

ISBNs: 9781923065093 (paperback)
                9781923065109 (ebook – epub)
                9781923065116 (ebook – Kindle)

Subjects: YOUNG ADULT FICTION / Historical / Ancient
                Civilizations; Science & Nature / Environment; Action &
                Adventure / General.

Cover concept by Charlotte Clutterbuck
Cover illustration by Lucinda Clutterbuck at www.piccolofilms.com.au
Other cover images used under licence from Adobe Stock.

Map created by Ruth Slater Artist at www.ruthslaterartist.com

TWIN STARS

VOLUME 1 OF *THE GANNET QUARTET*

CHARLOTTE CLUTTERBUCK

For

My sisters Harriet, Lucinda and Victoria

LANDS OF THE BEAR TRIBE

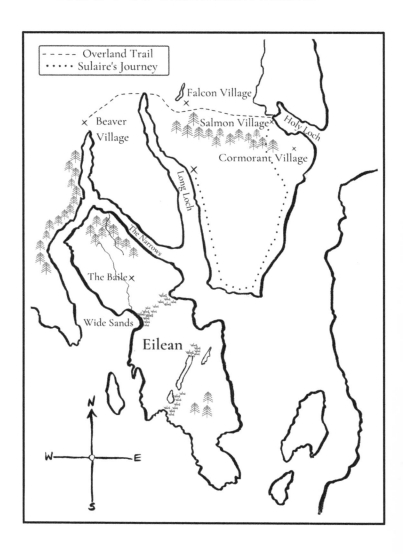

1

TWINS

AT THE SIGHT of the hazelnut husks on the deer-track, Bhòid flung down the bundle of rods he was carrying. If the nuts were ripe enough for the squirrels, they were ripe enough for him. Reaching into the bushes for a handful, he squatted on the track, cracking the small green nuts between two stones. They tasted milky on his tongue, but when he offered one to his twin sister Sulaire, she made a face and turned her head away.

'Too green yet,' she said, 'you'll give yourself a belly-ache.' She crouched beside him, drawing a pattern in the dust.

Bhòid went on cracking and eating nuts as he gathered a pile to take home to their mother. 'When I'm a Hunter,' he said, his mouth full, 'I'll sit all day in the sun eating nuts and raspberries while the village thralls carry the reeds and hazel-rods to mend *my* thatch.'

Sulaire tossed her head. 'You'll be a Hunter who's too lazy to go hunting.' She returned to her drawing, her face intent as the patterns swirled and interlaced.

'I'll be the greatest Hunter in the Beaver Clan. No, the greatest Hunter in the whole Tribe of the Bear. I'll kill many stags and have their antlers to decorate my house. I'll have such a strong totem—Wild Boar, perhaps—that no one will dare to even think I'm lazy if I sit in the sun eating berries.'

He thrust out his chin, daring her to contradict him, to say what their mother would have said—*Thralls can't have totems*—but Sulaire only looked up from her drawing with a grin. 'Your totem should be Squirrel,' she said.

'What would you know? I'll be Eagle or Wolf. I won't even flinch when they tattoo the Wolf symbol on my chest.'

Sulaire laughed, curling her hands into claws, rubbing her nose and chattering like a squirrel. 'You'll be a greedy little red squirrel, eating raw nuts before they're ripe.'

'Don't laugh, Sulaire. Don't mock the gods.'

'I wasn't laughing,' Sulaire said gravely. 'Well, I was, but I was laughing at you, not at the gods.'

With a quick but reverent gesture, she laid three nuts on a leaf under the bush. 'For you, Feorag,' she murmured and drew back a little. As if answering to its name, a red squirrel scuttered down from the bush, twitched its nose, picked up one of the nuts in its paws, flicked its flame of a tail and was gone.

'See?' Sulaire said, putting out one finger to touch the tip of his nose. 'It looked right at you. It knows what a little chatterer you are.'

'Squirrel!' Bhòid snorted. 'Squirrel's no totem for a Hunter. Just because it looked at me, it doesn't mean it's my totem. Anyway, what will yours be? Blue-tit perhaps. A blue-tit's tail feathers are just the colour of your eyes. A *baby* blue-tit.'

He thought she'd argue, even cuff him perhaps, but instead she gave him one of those distant looks of hers, as if she was seeing right through him; as if she was much older than their nine summers. As he stared at her, her eyes widened, filled with light, and Bhòid felt something beating—not a sound— barely a movement—a tremor in the air as if a great bird hovered above them and then was gone.

'Gannet,' he gasped, 'like your name, Sulaire.'

Her eyes darkened as if she was afraid, and she reached for his hand.

'What happened, Sulaire?'

She shook her head. 'It's not for me to say. Come on, Bhòid, it's going to rain.'

Hurriedly, the twins gathered up their bundle of rods, but long before they reached the village, the rain was lashing down against their faces. Thunder growled above the hills. *Perkwunos is angry*, thought Bhòid, hunching his shoulders and ducking his head against the stinging rain. *Are the gods angry that we talked about totems?*

The track grew slippery, and just as they reached the village, skirting the straggle of huts that surrounded the meeting-place, Bhòid's feet shot back out from under him and he fell face-first in the mud. He heard a jeering laugh, and across the meeting-place he saw Athru, the Headman's son, sitting in the doorway of his father's house, eating a honey cake, dry and comfortable in his warm jerkin of mountain-hare. He smirked as Bhòid struggled to his feet and wiped the mud from his face with the back of one hand.

'Athru,' muttered Bhòid angrily, as Sulaire helped him to gather up the scattered rods. 'Why doesn't Athru have to spend all day carrying bundles of rods for the thatches?'

'Because he's the Headman's son,' Sulaire murmured back. 'Because we're thralls.'

Dragging the rods inside their hut, the twins stripped off their tunics of tattered deer-hide and crouched naked and shivering while their mother tried to wake the fire with a handful of kindling that was damp because the roof leaked.

When I'm a Hunter, Bhòid thought, *I'll have a big house that doesn't leak, and I'll have plenty of furs and I'll eat meat for supper every night.* He could see himself—a tall Hunter with a sharp dagger and a carved antler pin fastening his wolf-hide cloak, daughters to stitch him warm winter jerkins and strong sons to stand behind him when he sat with the Great Ones of the Beaver Clan. The smoke from the sputtering fire made his eyes smart, and the vision faded. For now, he was a thrall, a thrall who didn't even know who his father was.

When Sulaire had scoured the pot after supper, she squatted beside Bhòid peeling the hazel-rods. Most evenings their mother was too tired to do more than finish the meal and sleep, but tonight, with the fresh nuts to thicken their stew of roots and herbs, a little colour returned to her pale cheeks. She sat by the twins, splitting the rods carefully into the flexible wands that would be used to renew the roof of the Headman's house.

As the thunder rumbled on she began to speak in a far-away voice, as if searching in her memory for a story, one of the stories that were told round the fire on winter nights when the whole Clan kept the wolf guard.

She told them how Sky God couldn't swim. He was afraid to go fishing in case Perkwunos the Thunder God capsized his boat, so he tied Perkwunos to a birch tree with magic bonds. First Mouse and First Dormouse both tried to gnaw through the magic rope and failed. But First Beaver chewed through the trunk until the tree fell and Perkwunos could slip out of his fetters.

Their mother made the twins laugh, imitating the mice squeaking, Beaver's teeth and furry voice, the Sky God's cloudy whisper, the roaring of Perkwunos, and the harsh cry and beating wings of the eagle who saved Sky God when Perkwunos upset his boat after all. Staring into the fire, Bhòid felt better—he was warm now, his belly full of stew, and his mother was telling a story. Perhaps the gods weren't angry after all.

Sulaire laid her head on their mother's knee. 'Mother,' she asked after a while, 'Who *is* our father? We must have one. Why won't you ever tell us?'

Their mother turned her head away, stroking Sulaire's hair, easing out the tangles with her fingers. Her voice, when she spoke, was bleak. 'When the salmon and the hazelnut harvest both failed in a single year, there was hunger all winter. At these times, the Great Ones choose a young woman of the Clan to travel up the traders' track to the nearest ford, and wait for the first man to come. A trader of red ochre was your father.'

'What was his name? Where did he come from?'

She shook her head. 'He didn't speak our language.'

'Was he kind?' asked Sulaire.

There was a long silence and then their mother said, 'He wasn't unkind.'

'When I'm a Hunter,' said Bhòid, 'I won't let the young women be sent out to the ford. I'll find another way.'

Their mother sighed. 'You won't be a Hunter, Bhòid. Thralls must work for the Hunters.'

'I'll find a way to be a Hunter.'

'Don't daydream, my son. The best thing for a thrall is to work hard. That way, you eat well and don't get beaten.'

When the twins were lying under their thin sleeping-hide, their mother snoring on the other side of the dying fire, Bhòid poked his sister gently. 'Sulaire, are you awake?'

'Mmm?'

'I *will* be a Hunter.'

'Of course,' she mumbled sleepily.

'And you, Sulaire? Will you be a Hunter with me, like the Moon Goddess and her Sun brother?'

'The Moon Goddess is also a Healer. I'll be a Healer.'

'But will you be a Hunter with me sometimes?'

She was quiet for so long that he thought she'd gone to sleep. 'I can't see hunting,' she said at last. 'I'm not a Hunter. I see us together all my life.'

'What do you mean, *see*?'

'Go to sleep, Bhòid.'

'What do you mean, all *your* life? What about all mine?'

'Go to sleep.'

'I will be a Hunter,' he insisted. 'When we start Cub training in the spring, I'll be so brave and clever they'll have to make me a Hunter. I'll be a great Hunter like Speir. Tell me the story of the Sky Twins, Sulaire.'

'Again?'

'Please.'

At first she spoke slowly, faltering, but as she told the familiar words, her voice strengthened.

Once, at the dawn of time, there were Twins, the boy Speir, and the girl Seren, children of the earth and the forest. Seren knew every blade of grass by the stream, and every flower on the heath, and every leaf in the forest. And Speir was the best hunter in the world, except for Ullr, the God of the Hunt.

One day when the Great Bear, Merak, was playing with Little Bear, Ullr the hunter came running with his spear and chased Little Bear far, far to the north. Merak called to the twins for help, and with Seren following the bent leaves, bruised flowers, and broken twigs of the trail, the Twins and Merak tracked Ullr for many days.

At last they saw Ullr ahead of them, but Ullr was drawing even closer to Little Bear. Then Speir flung his spear at Ullr with all his might, but Ullr was too quick for him and caught the spear and flung it aside. Just as Ullr raised his own spear to kill Little Bear, Speir dashed in front and Ullr drove the spear through him and Speir fell, dead.

Then Seren cried so many tears that she made a great river, and Merak feared that she would drown the whole world. So he took the Twins up and made them both into stars, standing beside the Sky River, and there they remain together, to this very day, the red star and the blue. And Merak was so angry with Ullr that he flung him to the far side of the Sky River where he cannot trouble the Twins.

Her voice quavered as she spoke the last lines.

'Why are you sad, Sulaire?' Bhòid asked.

'I'm just cold.' She shifted closer and laid her head against his shoulder.

'To this very day,' he murmured to himself. He could feel the warmth of her against him, the rhythm of her heart against his back as he drifted into sleep.

2

HANDS

SULAIRE WAITED ON the edge of the village meeting-place, shivering in the early spring morning. *At last*, she thought, *the Day of Balance when night and day are evenly matched and we are equal too—thrall and Hunter-caste equal as we train as Cubs of the Beaver Clan.* And yet her heart hammered in her chest. *Is it true?* she asked herself. *Is it true we are equal?*

Her stomach felt tight and empty. Neither she nor Bhòid had been able to eat—even the honey-cake their mother had made for this special morning had stuck in their throats, dry and crumbling.

Bhòid jiggled beside her, scuffing the dirt with his bare feet. He looked terribly young, younger than his nine summers, his dark hair ragged where their mother had cropped it to get rid of the tangles. His eyes darted around the village, looking for Athru, the Headman's son, tension in every muscle of his body.

The two girls who ran up to join them—Medjom, a thrall, and Lufar, a Hunter's daughter—were younger than Sulaire. She felt relieved when Lufar gave her a friendly grin and Medjom shyly took her hand and stood shifting on her bare feet as if she, too, was afraid. They'd be friends, Sulaire thought. At least, for the three years of Cubs training, they might be friends, whatever came later.

As Kolnos, the old Trainer who'd lost one eye in a wolf hunt, came across the meeting-place, his rawhide whip in his hand, he counted the four of them, and shook his head.

'Athru's mother is still doing his hair,' Lufar murmured to Sulaire, giggling. 'I did my own.' Sulaire looked down at her with a smile. Lufar's tunic was new, a pattern stitched at the neck, but her hair was simply combed and tied back with a thong.

When Athru joined the rest of the Cubs, he nodded casually to Kolnos and stood apart from the others in his fine clothes—a new doe-skin tunic, a jerkin trimmed with marten fur, otter-hide shoes laced at his ankles, his long black hair combed and plaited at the temples like a Hunter's.

And Sulaire realised the truth: *Athru will not think that he and Bhòid are equals. There are only two boys and Athru will be Headman one day. He will think he is better than Bhòid. They will be rivals, not friends.*

Kolnos led the Cubs into the woods for their first day's training. Old as he was, he was tough. He ran the Cubs in a zig-zag path from stream to deer-track, across rocks, through fern and tussock, uphill and down. Her chest burning, Sulaire strained to keep up with his steady jog. Just as she thought she could run no longer, she realised that she was closest to the old man, Bhòid and Medjom panting close behind her. Lufar and Athru—not hardened by work like the thrall-children—were falling back. She could see trouble if Bhòid beat Athru. She stopped suddenly, dropping forward, hands on knees, as if she had a stitch. Medjom stumbled into her, but Bhòid side-stepped and ploughed on. Athru slogged behind him, his breath coming in whistling gasps, but it was Bhòid who reached Kolnos first as the old man halted on the edge of the wood, looking over the moors. Sulaire saw the hot, angry look in Athru's eyes, and knew she was right. He would not take kindly to Bhòid beating him at anything.

As Kolnos passed the water-skin he carried first to Athru and then to Lufar, Sulaire wondered if the old trainer would be fair.

Trying to stop worrying, Sulaire turned away from the group. She stood transfixed by the rolling open space. She'd never been so high before, never seen the dry clumps of heather, grey as the open sea on a cloudy day, the wind riffling through them in waves. She felt at home here, just as she did by the edge of the sea, watching the gannets diving. A splash of purple caught her eye and she dropped to one knee, stretching out a finger to touch the clump of flowers blooming amongst the roots of the heather. She put a single flower into her mouth, exploring it with her tongue. It tasted sweet.

It must be good for something, she thought, but when she plucked another flower and showed it to Kolnos, he merely shrugged. 'Saxifrage,' he said and turned away to watch the others, who lay, still red-faced and panting, amongst the ferns.

'Saxifrage,' she repeated, as if naming the plant would let her hear its secrets. She ate the second flower and felt a tingling in her mouth. A clean freshness.

She would have gathered more, but Kolnos was already signalling the Cubs to get up.

'In another moon or so,' he said, smiling grimly, 'we'll see what you're really made of.' As Kolnos led the way into the woods, Athru shoved Bhòid aside and followed Kolnos first down the narrow track, flinging his plaits back over his shoulders.

Sulaire held a batten steady as old Thorn, the best thatcher of the village, fastened it over the bundles of sea-grass below it. All through the summer afternoon, Sulaire and the other girls—light and agile—had crawled over the Headman's roof, helping Thorn. When the battens were all lashed down, he showed them how to lay and tie down the next course of bundles. Of all the tasks that the Cubs were learning, Sulaire almost liked thatching best—the smell of the sea-grass, the sun on her back, the fine work that made her fingers strong and supple. Every so often she'd pause and look from this high perch over the village, down the slope, to the estuary beyond.

She sneezed. The work was hot and dusty, and when Thorn packed up his tools, the three girls ran gladly down to the burn, washed and splashed, and then, in the long summer evening, sat on the bank, picking the lice out of each other's hair.

'Kolnos works the boys too hard,' said Medjom.

'Well, he works your brother too hard, Sulaire.'

Sulaire glanced back towards the Headman's house. Kolnos, his whip slung over his shoulder, was watching Bhòid and Athru as they carried bundles of sea-grass from the drying sheds and stacked them ready for Thorn to use in the morning. Even from here, Sulaire could see that Bhòid was gathering more bundles into a load, moving faster, stacking them more carefully. Yet it was Bhòid that Kolnos flicked on his bare legs when he paused to catch his breath. When Athru fell to one knee and made a great show of tying his shoe-strings, Kolnos looked the other way.

It had been like this all summer. Late in the spring, the Headman Fiada, with his woman and his chosen Hunters had clambered into their great canoes and paddled away to the three-month summer Gathering of the Bear Tribe. Those left behind—Kolnos and the small band of Hunters who'd oversee the summer's work—were quick with their whips when they thought the Cubs and thralls weren't working hard enough.

'See,' said Medjom, as Athru finished tying his shoe and slowly gathered another bundle of sea-grass while Kolnos did nothing to hurry him.

Lufar shrugged. 'Of course. Athru's the Headman's son. He will be a Hound and then a Hunter and then Headman in his turn. That's the Custom.'

Medjom turned her freckled face towards Sulaire. 'Aren't we all equals? Until we're trained and the gods choose our paths—who will go on to Hounds training with the Tribe, and who will just stay here in the village as thralls?'

Sulaire shook her head. 'I don't know,' she said slowly, and Lufar, who never quite forgot that she was a Hunter's daughter, looked at her pointedly, daring her to question the Custom. 'I don't know,' Sulaire said again.

'Mightn't any of us be chosen Hunter or thrall?' persisted Medjom, her eyes pleading. 'Or is it all a lie? Is there no hope for us?'

Doubt rose in Sulaire's mind. *What if the gods have already decided? What if no one thrall-born can ever be a Hunter? What if Bhòid's dreams are hopeless, as mother says?* She shook off the thought. *Surely the gods aren't so cruel.* She took Medjom by the hand. 'It's for the gods to decide,' she said. Then she smiled, 'And for us, now, it's time for another swim.'

As Medjom and Lufar plunged back into the water, Sulaire paused on the edge. She noticed that while Kolnos let Athru go as soon as he'd dumped his next bundle, he sent Bhòid to fetch a last load, though Bhòid had already carried far more than Athru.

She remembered how each morning, when Kolnos reminded the Cubs of the Balance, sometimes the old man with the wolf-scarred face spoke as if the words were worn thin with repetition:

Take only one egg from the nest, hunt the old and the weak so the herd remains strong, let the salmon run free at full moon.

This wasn't the first time she'd thought that Kolnos was one-eyed in spirit. With only two boys to train, Kolnos couldn't help pitting them against each other, but he might have made sure it was a fair fight. With his longer arms, Athru could punch Bhòid in the face and split his lip, or wrestle Bhòid to the ground, put a knee in his back, twisting his neck in a headlock. And instead of helping Bhòid, showing him some tricks, perhaps, Kolnos set them to hand-to-hand combat nearly every day, almost as if he enjoyed watching Bhòid take a beating.

Where's the Balance in that? Sulaire wondered, but it made her feel almost sick to ask. She must believe in the Balance—the force that weighed life and death, good and evil, strong and weak—the guardian of fairness. 'I do believe,' she whispered to the sky, as she drew herself up at the edge of the stream before diving in.

On the morning after the Headman Fiada's return from the Gathering that autumn, he wandered over to watch the Cubs. He was impressive, thought Sulaire, tall for a Beaver, an air of contained strength in his stillness as he stood at the edge of the fighting circle. Instead of the Hunters' plaits and adornments, he wore a simple tunic and his hair cut short, already grizzled at the temples.

First the girls went through their paces—walking on their hands, cartwheels, somersaults—the moves needed for the young women's

Dance of Plenty that kept the Moon and the Sun turning the seasons. Sulaire felt the thrill of her body swinging and twisting through the air, almost like a bird in flight. When she stopped and the world steadied around her, she sensed that Fiada was watching her appraisingly.

Then it was the boys' turn, Bhòid and Athru, hand-to-hand, best of three.

Bhòid hurled himself into the first bout, fists flailing, desperate to show Fiada that he was worthy of being a Hunter. But Athru landed a punch on Bhòid's chest, knocked him flying and leaped on top, grinding Bhòid's face into the dust until Kolnos, taking rather longer than was needed, blew his bone whistle to end the bout.

Bhòid's nose was bleeding as he walked stiffly back to the edge of the circle. Sulaire fished out a short twig that she kept in her pouch in case of nose-bleeds and gave it to him to clench between his teeth. When the bleeding stopped, Bhòid stood glaring across the circle at Athru.

'Use what you have,' came a deep voice beside her. Startled, Sulaire glanced up to see Fiada looking down at Bhòid with a faint smile in his clear blue eyes. 'Use everything you have, not just courage.'

Bhòid wiped the last trickle of blood from his nose and stared at Fiada.

'Think. What do you have that he lacks?'

'Speed?'

'And?'

Bhòid shook his head.

'Agility, perhaps?' Fiada said, with a sideways glance at Sulaire. 'You're built like your sister. Take your time. Don't dash in.'

When Bhòid stared at him, Fiada jerked his head impatiently at the circle.

This time Bhòid entered the circle slowly, crouched, moving sideways like a crab, keeping just out of Athru's reach. Surprised, Athru swung round after him. Bhòid moved a little faster, weaving left, right, darting in only to leap back out of range. Until, out of patience, Athru ran at him. At the last moment, Bhòid side-stepped, landing a light blow on Athru's shoulder. Athru turned, yelling, and ran back at him. This time, just as he side-stepped, Bhòid thrust out one foot, kicked Athru's shin out from under him, and the bigger boy fell. In a flash, Bhòid was on him, but Athru, heavier, twisted furiously in his grasp and flung him off.

'Enough for today!' Fiada spoke with quiet authority as he pulled them apart. 'One bout to each of you. Now Kolnos and I will show you a few tricks. Slowly. Without anger. For learning.'

In a measured dance, the two men played out the moves so that the Cubs could see the holds and trips, the breakaways, and how to fall.

When Fiada turned to leave, he tapped Bhòid lightly on the shoulder. 'Courage,' he said, 'and now some skill. Good.' He smiled at Sulaire. 'And a sister who knows how to tend the hurts your courage earns you.'

As he turned away, Sulaire saw the look Athru gave Bhòid. He'd been beaten in front of his father, even if only in one bout, and things would be worse now for Bhòid.

Autumn passed, winter, spring, and summer, and Athru hadn't forgiven Bhòid. It was small things, mainly—a log dropped so that it fell on Bhòid's toe; a blade that slipped and gashed Bhòid's arm— nothing that Athru could be blamed for. He always did just enough work to avoid Kolnos's lash.

'Don't try to beat him, Bhòid,' said Sulaire. 'Let him win if it's so important.'

She watched her brother learn to hold back in running, to cast his spear less accurately, to submit quickly at hand-to-hand, and to excel only with the sling, which Athru despised as a thrall's weapon. And she wondered what the holding back might be doing to Bhòid's spirit.

Again the seasons passed, and they entered their third year. The Cubs had learned the spoor and scat of every animal, how to read wind and tide, use saw and axe and adze. They could make fire even when it was raining, finding dry tinder under overhangs and scrub, peeling twigs to expose the dry wood inside, working fire-board and drill in the shelter of a tree. Only on the bleakest days would Kolnos gruffly uncover the smouldering tinder fungus he carried in a horn, allowing them to blow on it to bring the fire to life.

And still Athru looked down on Bhòid, and still Kolnos favoured Athru.

'You'd think it would be Fiada who favoured Athru,' Bhòid muttered one night, as Sulaire crouched beside him in the hut, rubbing heather liniment into his wrenched shoulder.

Sulaire felt for the knots in his shoulder, kneading

and pushing, as if she could ease Bhòid's unhappiness as well as his strained muscles. 'Fiada wants Athru to be truly strong in himself,' she said. 'Not to win by tricking and bullying. He wants to leave the Clan in good hands when he dies.'

'And Kolnos?'

'Any of us, even Fiada, could die any day—by wolf or fever or accident. Kolnos is getting old. He wants to know that the next Headman will be grateful to him.'

'If the next Headman's Athru, we'll run away.'

Her hands froze, the fire wavered before her eyes and seemed to fade. Something—not as sharp as vision—a sense, a shadow, a dream-image of a boy running—*Bhòid alone and running for his life.* She caught her breath as the sharp scent of bog myrtle hung from the roof to dry brought her back to herself.

'What's wrong, Sulaire?'

'Nothing,' she said, but even as the image faded, it left something behind, a tingling in her fingers. She rubbed vigorously at her brother's shoulder, almost as if to anchor herself, and felt the heat come into her hands and surge into his skin.

He twisted his head to look at her. 'Sulaire?'

'What?'

'How do you know what to do? Your hands feel so much better than mother's.'

She stared down at her hands, strong with work, brown with sun, as if she'd never seen them before. 'They tell me what to do,' she said. 'Almost as if they're not my hands—as if it comes from somewhere else.' She broke off. The image of her brother running came back to her. 'Bhòid,' she said urgently, 'don't make an enemy of Athru.'

'I've tried. It's not me. It's him. He hates me. I only want to be friends, but he hates me.'

'Perhaps he sees something in you that he lacks. Keep trying, Bhòid. Try harder. Find something you can do for him. Perhaps the Autumn Hunt. Don't beat him in the Autumn Hunt.'

'Sulaire!' he protested. 'I must be First Spear. Kolnos must see what I can do. He must give me my totem.'

3

THE MARKING

THE AFTERNOON BEFORE the Autumn Hunt, when all his tasks were done, there was still enough light for Bhòid to run down to the training-ground and practise hurling his throw-spear into a clump of grass as if it was a young buck. Tomorrow, the buck would be real, and when he killed it, Kolnos would make the marks of First Spear on his forehead.

As the evening light glowed on the yellowing birch trees, he walked back up the hill and saw Athru sitting at the edge of the meeting-place, intent on something in his hands, rubbing it carefully, almost stroking. As Bhòid came closer, Athru paused in polishing the knife he held—a new knife that Fiada must have given him for his first hunt—and held it so that Bhòid could see. It was a beautiful thing, green-grey flint, leaf-shaped, with fine ridges where the knapper had struck off flakes of stone. The last light played over it like running water over pebbles.

Bhòid put out one finger and touched the blade, almost reverently. The boys' eyes met, and for a moment Athru dropped his guard. They stood there sharing the wonder of the knife and the knowledge of the coming test, and Bhòid had a sudden sense of what it might be like if they could be friends.

'Are you scared?' Bhòid asked, his own fear and excitement wrangling in his chest like a pair of pine martens fighting.

Athru stared at him. Bhòid could see an answering flicker of fear in his eyes, before a blankness came down like the hide curtain over a house door. Athru tossed his head, thrust the knife back into its sheath, and turned away.

In the first glimmer of dawn, the Cubs crouched in the scrub, motionless, throw-spears at the ready, spears that Kolnos had blessed before they left the village and sprinkled with sacred water. As the light grew, they saw the herd of young bucks, and Kolnos raised his hand. The Cubs shot from cover, sending the herd galloping away from them towards the birch copse where the Hunters waited in ambush.

As Bhòid raced across the heath—the girls strung out on his right, Athru pounding on his left—he felt all the exultation of speed and quickened his pace, leaving Athru running heavily in his wake.

Ahead of him, the Hunters leaped from behind the trees and the startled herd churned into a panic of milling beasts, caught between the two groups. As the Cubs closed in behind, Bhòid flung his spear. Too early. It fell short, useless, and there was no time to swerve and pick it up. How could he be First Spear now, without a spear?

Without thinking, he snatched the sling from his belt and a stone from his pouch, chose his target—a young buck on the edge of the herd—and cast. A glancing blow to the head that half-stunned but didn't kill.

As the deer buckled at the knees, Athru darted in, thrusting his spear into the deer's flank, and it fell. He tried to slit the creature's throat with his new knife, but it was his first kill, and messy, and Kolnos stooped, drew his own knife, and in a flash it was over. As Kolnos yanked Athru to his feet,

Bhòid realised that something was wrong. Kolnos was staring from one boy to the other, the blood drained from his face.

Bhòid stared back at Kolnos, not under-standing, and then he knew. *First Spear*. It was supposed to be First Spear, not first sling-stone. A sling was a thrall's weapon. He'd used it in the sacred hunt and now Athru was looking at him with hatred because his kill was tainted.

The three of them stood there as if even Kolnos didn't know what to do. The Hunt was over now, the Hunters finishing off their kills as the rest of the herd fled on up the hill. With a sick feeling in his stomach, Bhòid waited until Fiada strode up and asked, 'What happened?'

Athru couldn't look at his father. Bhòid took a step forward and held out his sling. 'I dropped my spear,' he faltered. 'So I used my sling.'

'I was First Spear,' Athru almost wailed, 'and now it's ruined.'

Kolnos cut in. 'It's the Custom,' he said 'the sacred Custom that keeps the deer-herd strong. Only spears, spears that have been blessed. Bhòid is taboo. Two days in the punishment hut.'

Bhòid nodded dumbly. He knew about the

punishment hut. No food, no water till the taboo was lifted.

Fiada shook his head. 'Both boys acted without thought. Bhòid shouldn't have used a sling, but if Athru hadn't finished the kill, the buck might have lived. Both boys are taboo. They must learn to control themselves, even in the heat of the chase.' His face softened a little. 'They're boys, only twelve summers. A day and a night. Until mid-morning tomorrow.'

Kolnos looked as if he wanted to protest, but Fiada merely nodded and turned away. Two Hunters took the boys back down the hill to the village, pushed them into the hut, and barred the door behind them.

It was dark inside. Nothing but the bare floor and a small latrine with a pile of dirt beside it in one corner. Bhòid squatted on the ground, arms round his knees. He could almost smell Athru's rage as he shifted restlessly at the far end of the hut. It was not yet mid-morning and the day that had started with such promise was spoiled. He had spoilt it.

'I'm sorry,' Bhòid said. He heard Athru spit, but he knew Athru wouldn't dare to hurt him.

There must be no fighting in the hut. There was nothing to do but wait.

Bhòid had failed in the Autumn Hunt, but he wouldn't think about that. He would not. If he bore his punishment well, the gods would forgive him. There was still the wolf guard. Still time to show his courage. *Ullr*, he prayed, *forgive me. I didn't mean to flout the Custom.*

The long day passed. He'd had nothing to eat or drink since before dawn and his mouth was parched, but he must have fallen asleep, because he was woken by the smell of roasting meat and the sound of voices singing and shouting—the Hunters round the fire, feasting. He heard sniffling, and realised Athru was crying. Cautiously he felt his way to the end of the hut and put out his hand.

'Are you cold?' he asked. 'If we lie side by side, it will be better.' Athru shoved him away. Bhòid crawled back to the other end of the hut and sat against the wall, listening to Athru's stifled sobs. 'You'll make yourself thirstier,' Bhòid said. After a while, Athru's sobs died away. It was near midnight, but Bhòid couldn't sleep. He felt light-headed and a cold wind was blowing through the cracks in the hut. From time to time, Athru groaned, but Bhòid crouched silently, staring into the gloom, moving as little as possible, enduring.

It seemed a long time later when he heard a faint rustling outside the hut, a voice, hardly audible in the wind, 'Athru.' A woman's voice, he thought. His ears sharpened by the time in the darkness, Bhòid could hear faint sounds at the door, as if the bar was being lifted with infinite care, a creak. Then the sound of Athru gulping. Water. Bhòid felt rather than heard another movement—Athru feeling for him in the darkness.

'Water,' Athru whispered.

Bhòid took a deep breath. Every part of his body called for the water. But if he broke the taboo, how could the gods help him? Carefully, so as not to spill the water, Bhòid pushed Athru's hand away.

'Water,' Athru insisted.

'I won't tell,' Bhòid croaked, 'but I won't drink.' He listened to the movement—Athru retreating, the creak of the door, the faintest of thuds as the bar dropped, then silence.

Bhòid sat motionless in the darkness. He tried to lick his lips, but there was no moisture on his tongue.

'You don't understand,' Athru said. 'My mother lost three sons before me. She's frightened I'll get sick and die too. She'll make an offering so the gods won't be angry.' It was almost as if he was pleading with Bhòid.

Bhòid croaked again, 'I won't tell.' He lay in the darkness, trying to sleep, trying to make the time go faster, but his head ached and his eyes felt dry and gritty. He must have slept a little, for when he woke, he heard sounds of movement in the village and knew that dawn had come. Still the time dragged through the morning until at last the door opened. The two boys staggered to their feet and stood blinking in the light. Two Hunters half led, half dragged them down to the pool in the stream where Fiada and Kolnos were waiting to oversee the ritual cleansing. Plunging into the water, Bhòid sucked up great gulps of it, washed himself all over and came up dripping.

'You are clean, now,' Fiada said, putting his hands on the boys' heads in the gesture of forgiveness. 'Respect the Custom.'

As Fiada turned to go, Bhòid glanced at Athru and saw the look in his eye. Ashamed, afraid.

Winter came early that year. Weeks of snow were followed by bright days, nights blazing with stars and bitter cold that froze the streams and the ground and even the edge of the sea. Afterwards, more snow. The Beavers hacked ice from the stream and melted it for drinking, and every day they had to go further in search for firewood or to set snares for what game remained.

Long before the end of winter, the wolves howled in the forest, coming a little closer every night. Above the village, where the wolves were most likely to come out of the woods, the Beavers lit a great fire every night. Nearby were stacks of throw-spears, small fires laid ready for lighting if the wolves came, pine-pitch torches and piles of stones for the slingers. Night after night they waited, but the wolves didn't attack. Until one night, the howling grew even closer and they knew the wolves were coming.

All Bhòid's childhood he'd imagined crouching, spear poised, ready to fling it at the wolves—another chance to show his worthiness to be a Hunter. Now that the time was here, now that he could hear the wolves' plaintive cries coming closer and closer, his heart was thudding and he could hardly breathe. He had no spear. Kolnos had taken the Cubs' spears to add to the stacks for the thralls to use. All they had were their slings and a small pile of stones. Just in case.

'Keep well back,' Kolnos had said, 'You're not strong or skilled enough to be useful. Stay back. Watch and learn. Try to get used to the stink of them.' Then he'd gone to join the main band of Hunters.

The wind sharpened and the howling grew closer still. A thrall lit a torch at the great fire, and as he ran along the curve of the forward defence, thrusting his torch into each of the smaller fires, the flames leaped into the dark night.

Beside Bhòid, Sulaire crouched, tense and shivering. Clutching his sling, a stone in one palm ready to load, Bhòid grasped her hand. 'Stay behind me. Whatever happens.' She shook her head, her face a wild mask of red and shadows in the firelight, and stayed where she was. Bhòid glanced across at Athru and saw him nervously licking his lips.

The wolves slipped out of the woods, moving over the snow in a loose pack of shadows, closer, closer. The thralls leaped out from the wings of the line of defence, waving torches, slinging stones, flinging throw-spears, and the wolves bunched together and drew back.

The night seemed to hold its breath. Again the wolves came on, weaving and snaking across the snow, looking for weak points in the defence, approaching, retreating, darting forwards. Again the thralls whirled torches and set up a wild clamour on the flanks of the pack, funnelling the wolves towards the small band of Hunters who leaped to meet them—nine men with heavy strong-bladed thrusting spears.

Bhòid crouched with the Cubs, staring at the wild mass of tumbling, snapping, thrusting and struggling—wolves and men, torches, spears.

He heard Sulaire's voice beside him, shouting *'Bhòid!'*, turned and saw—less than a spear-throw away—a wolf swinging away from the pack, slinking towards them. Filled with terror, Bhòid looked round desperately for Kolnos, but the old man was busy with the main pack. Bhòid rose to his feet, grabbing a stone. He tried to shout to the others, 'Don't turn! Don't run!' but his voice stuck in this throat. On his left, Sulaire and the girls were already fitting stones to their slings. On his right, Athru was tugging at his knife. Half a spear-throw away, the wolf came on steadily. It was huge, its shoulders more massive than any of the village dogs. Bhòid started to whirl his sling, but his hands shook and the stone dropped uselessly behind him. He snatched another stone from his pouch and cast. The stone bounced off the thick fur of the wolf's shoulder and still it came on. The wolf's rank smell was in his nostrils, and he took a step back, aware of the others beside him also falling back.

Out of the corner of his eye, he saw Fiada come leaping towards them, spear in one hand, torch in the other, Kolnos panting behind. As Fiada thrust with his spear, the wolf twisted away and ran. The whole pack was running now, thralls and Hunters harrying their flanks.

Now that it was over, the girls huddled together, crying with relief. Bhòid dropped to the ground, shivering and gasping. He hadn't known he could be so afraid. Beside him, his hands shaking, Athru stared at the knife in his hands as if he'd never seen it before.

Fiada looked down the terrified Cubs. His face was streaked with sweat and soot, blood dripping from a gash on his arm onto the snow. Grasping his son by the shoulder, he snapped, 'A knife! What were you thinking of? Where was your sling?'

He looked from Cub to Cub, 'What were you doing, so close?'

Kolnos said nothing to defend them.

Fiada went on, disgust in every word. 'Next time, stay in your place. Do as you're told! Children! Get back to your beds.' He turned on his heel and stalked back to the main band where already men were dragging three dead wolves down towards the village.

Suddenly Athru turned aside and vomited. His own stomach churning, Bhòid reached out to hold Athru's hair back from his face, but Athru snarled at him and Bhòid dropped his hand.

As the twins walked back towards their hut, Bhòid said, 'Athru was afraid.'

'Weren't you?'

'Terrified. But it was worse for him.'

'You were just afraid. He was afraid of his fear.'

'I don't understand.'

'He's afraid his fear will get the better of him,' Sulaire said, 'afraid he'll disgrace himself. That he's not fit to be Headman after Fiada.'

'Fiada's usually so fair. Except for tonight. We stayed where we were told. We even held our ground.'

'He was afraid, too. He felt bad it had happened. He was afraid for Athru.'

'Yes,' said Bhòid slowly. 'Did you know that Fiada lost three sons before Athru was born?'

'No.'

'When Athru told me that in the punishment hut, I thought we might become friends, but he still hates me.'

'Fear makes him angry,' Sulaire said, 'and sometimes cruel. He's afraid of too many things; not just wolves. His father. Himself.'

At last, in their twelfth spring, the Day of Totems came. All day Kolnos and the Cubs scoured the woods and heathland, waiting for the totems to show themselves, but the spring day passed without sign. At dusk they crouched behind a hazel copse, waiting in case a badger came out.

Beside him, Bhòid could sense Athru quivering with tension. He felt his own dread growing. Badger wouldn't be the totem he'd dreamed of—not Wolf or Eagle or Boar—but it would be a totem. What if no totem came? None at all?

A nightjar churred, but still the badger didn't come out to feed. It was the last day of training and now they were almost out of time. Tomorrow on the Day of Balance, those the gods had chosen would be given their totem mark, and those who weren't … he pushed the thought away.

When the dusk was long faded and only the glimmer of starlight made strange shadows in the woods, Kolnos raised his hand, and the Cubs slipped silently down the hill. Bhòid strained to hear the rustling of animals, a scream when some night creature caught its prey. They travelled home so slowly that the moon rose, on the wane, showing more clearly the pale track threading through the dark scrub.

Bhòid smelt it first—the musky smell of a bear. He froze, every nerve quivering with wishing. *Let it be for me, Oh Merak, Great Bear, choose me.* Crashing and huffing, the bear burst out of the bushes and crossed the path between Kolnos and Athru. Athru stood fixed to the spot. As the bear lifted its head and looked at Athru, Bhòid saw a flash of moving silver—a salmon, still alive, thrashing in the bear's mouth. The bear growled and was gone.

Moments later a barn owl glided shrieking overhead, its face glimmering white in the moonlight. Kolnos gave a satisfied grunt, and moved off, leading them briskly back to the village—as if two totems were enough.

'Who did they choose?' Bhòid whispered desperately to Sulaire.

'Not us,' she breathed. 'It's as mother said. Totems don't choose thralls. The bear walked in front of Athru, and he held still.'

'He was too terrified to move. And the owl flew over you.'

'Between me and Lufar. Kolnos will have seen it over Lufar's head.'

'He sees what he wants to see.'

'He's bound by the Custom. Have you ever seen a thrall with a totem?'

It came to Bhòid with full force. Totems were for Hunters. Tomorrow, after the Marking, he would truly be a thrall. Athru would go to this year's Gathering of the Bear Tribe, with the powerful totem of Bear, and Bhòid would stay here, a thrall of the Beaver Clan. He stifled a sob as he felt Sulaire's hand searching for his in the darkness.

Much later, as he was drifting into sleep, he found himself asking how the salmon was there at all. Yes, salmon came sometimes in spring, but not often to the Beaver Burn.

Next day, the five Cubs fasted and cleansed themselves. In the evening Kolnos led them to the meeting-place where the whole Clan was gathered around the fire. The skin of Bhòid's scalp tingled as he watched the waiting faces.

First, Kolnos signalled Medjom and Sulaire to come to the fire, shaved the hair from their right temple and took a piece of charcoal to make the thrall-mark on their skin, where each girl would renew it every morning until, one day, perhaps, a Hunter took her as his woman, and she never had to make it again. Kolnos raised his voice and spoke to the waiting Beavers, 'These girls are ready to serve the Beaver Clan.' The Clan drummed their feet on the ground in acknowledgement, but as Sulaire came back to stand beside him, Bhòid couldn't meet her eyes.

When Kolnos beckoned to him, Bhòid pulled his hair back, walked firmly to the fire, knelt and turned his face towards Kolnos. *Hold still*, he willed himself.

Don't flinch. Show them. The old man took a brand from the fire and brought its glowing end closer and closer to his left temple—a smell of smoke—a searing pain—the stench of burned flesh—tears starting from his eyes, the world spinning before him. But he hadn't flinched. Kolnos spoke again, 'This boy is ready to serve the Beaver Clan.'

Kolnos reached a hand to help him to his feet, looking at Bhòid as if he'd never seen him before, almost regretfully. Bhòid heard the Clan drumming their feet faster and fiercer, acknowledging his courage as he walked as steadily as he could to join the other thralls.

Then Kolnos took Athru and Lufar by the hand. 'The White Owl has chosen this daughter, and Merak has chosen this son. They are ready now for their training as Hounds of the Bear Tribe.'

As Athru and Lufar knelt before Fiada, he took a knife and nicked them lightly on the breastbone so that a few drops of blood fell onto the totem pendants they held. These he placed round their necks, an owl's skull for Lufar, a bear's claw for Athru. Later, when they'd showed themselves worthy of the Tribe, their totem marks would be tattooed on their chests.

The moon was not yet risen as Bhòid stumbled blindly away from the fire, not knowing quite where he was going—somewhere, anywhere, away. *Never, never, never,* hammered the burn throbbing on his temple.

As he neared the edge of the village, he heard footsteps hurrying behind him, and sensed, rather than saw, that his mother was coming behind him. 'What did I say?' she muttered under her breath. 'Thralls can never become Hunters. Even if they're as brave as my son.' She reached out her hand, but he knew that if he let her touch him he'd start blubbering like a baby. 'Bhòid,' she said, 'come home. Please.' Shrugging, keeping his distance, he followed her back to the hut. What else was there to do?

After the Marking, boys slept on the men's side of the fire. While Sulaire salved Bhòid's burn, their mother spread his sleeping-hide on the other side of their small fire. He moved across and lay down, the brand blistering on his temple. The brand where hair would never grow. All the clans of the Bear Tribe, perhaps all the clans beyond, marked their thralls like this. There was nowhere for him to escape. Wherever he ran, he was marked.

Never, never, never! pulsed the wound. He could never be a Hunter now.

Tears trickled down the side of his nose. As he lay there, shuddering, he sensed the faintest slither of movement, an arm coming over his shoulder, Sulaire burrowing her face into his back.

'Don't the spirits care about us?' Bhòid whispered.

'Believe in them.' She breathed the words quietly into his ear. 'Maybe they'll give us totems, even if we are thralls.'

'How will they know we believe?'

'Speak to them. In your heart, Bhòid. Make a ceremony. There must be more for us than this. Believe.'

'I believe. I believe. I believe,' he repeated to himself, like wavelets lapping on the loch-shore above the steady drubbing of the pain.

4

SEEING

ONE CLEAR MORNING, before the first rim of light showed in the east, before the village was stirring, Sulaire woke Bhòid and they stole away up the burn. As the first glimmer of sunlight touched the young leaves, she chose a flat rock near the water. The twins lit a small fire with the smouldering tinder fungus Sulaire had brought packed in a hollow bone. Then she threw an offering of hazelnuts into the fire.

'There should be blood,' Bhòid said.

'Not on the breastbone. Not where the others were marked.' Sulaire plucked two dock leaves, found a sharp stone and chose a spot on Bhòid's collarbone, near his right shoulder where no one would know it for a Totem Mark. No one must know that the twins had dared to make the sacred mark for themselves. She cut his brown skin carefully, collecting a few drops of blood on the leaf. When she handed him the shell, he hesitated. 'Here,' she said, guiding his hand to her shoulder. He gritted his teeth and pushed the shell a little too hard. Blood sprang out onto the leaf in her hand, a small pool of red.

Dipping her finger into the blood, Sulaire drew three wavy lines on Bhòid's forehead— marks of no totem, but sacred all the same, marks of sea or wind. He did the same for her. She found a cobweb glittering between two bushes and used some to stop the bleeding on her collarbone.

Then she turned to the fire, suddenly shy, and raised her arms, searching for the words.

'Great Spirits,' she blurted.

—Of the Wood—

—And the Sky—

—And the Water—

—The Sea—

—Fire—

—Wind—

'Spirits of Seren and Speir,' they spoke together, 'Guide us. Show us our totems.'

They dropped their leaves in the fire, watched them shrivel into flakes of black, waited until the fire burned down before covering the embers with earth, washing the blood from their foreheads.

'Do you think they heard us?' Bhòid asked.

'Be patient,' she said. 'They're waiting.'

'What for?'

'To see who we are. What we can do. To know us before they can choose us.'

Perched high in the branches of a sycamore, Sulaire could hear the sound of adzes ringing on timber. On the shore below the village, thralls were shaping the canoe that would carry Fiada to the Gathering. She was glad to be up here, gathering birds' eggs, far from the noise, the sticky task of heating resin and beeswax for glue, the endless sanding of paddles.

Bhòid whistled to her from an ash tree a little further up the hill, and she whistled back, watching the movement of the leaves as he climbed higher.

She looked out across the estuary and wondered what it would be like to travel to the Gathering, the boat lifting over the waves beneath her. She'd never been in a boat. Boats were for the Great Ones of the Clan to travel in. Most likely, if she ever did go to the Gathering, she'd travel overland with the other thralls, carrying furs to trade.

Raising herself carefully from her perch, Sulaire reached towards the nest above her. Just as her hand found three warm, rounded shapes, she heard a crack, a cry, a crashing through branches, then a thud. Forgetting the eggs, slithering to the ground as fast as she dared, she ran towards the clump of ferns beneath the ash. When she reached Bhòid, his upper arm was lying at a crooked angle, his eyes were closed and his skin had a greenish tinge. His eyes fluttered open, but she could see that he was barely conscious.

She knelt beside him, her own head swimming. As she felt his arm, his eyes opened and he whimpered. 'Bite on this,' she said, giving him a birch twig. 'Try not to move.' Probing with her fingers, she felt the sharp edge of bone beneath flesh. *I don't know what to do*, she thought. *We didn't learn this. Bind it*, she thought, *like a wrenched ankle? No, something stronger.*

Searching the undergrowth, she found comfrey leaves and two sticks. There were strips of hide in her pouch. 'Be still,' she said, as she started to work. He clenched his teeth, but every now and then as she wrapped his arm in comfrey leaves and bound it to the sticks, a groan escaped. When she'd finished, he rolled over and vomited into the ferns.

She fetched water from the burn in her pouch, slopped some into his mouth, and washed his face and neck with the wet leather. Then she made a rough sling with her belt and helped him back to the village.

When they reached the healing hut, Ead, Wise Woman of the Clan, looked them up and down. Sulaire could feel how ragged and dirty they must both look. 'When I heal someone,' Ead said, 'there's payment—a marten fur or a pair of fresh-killed hares, for something like this.'

'We're thralls,' Bhòid mumbled. 'We have nothing.'

'Thralls heal as best they can. It will heal. A bit short, but it will heal.'

'It's my right arm!'

Sulaire gazed up at Ead. 'I will work for you, Teacher,' she offered, 'I'll come before and after my other tasks and do whatever you tell me.'

'How old are you?'

'Nearly thirteen summers.'

Ead shook her head.

'I know many of the plants on the hills,' Sulaire said urgently. 'I'll go out at first light and gather them fresh. I'll do the filthiest tasks. Please, Teacher.'

Ead looked at her as if sizing her up. 'Very well,' she said, pointing to the rough table in her hut. Sulaire helped Bhòid onto the table, and, since Ead seemed to expect it, she unwrapped Bhòid's arm. Ead passed her a cup of dark liquid, and she held it to Bhòid's lips, smelling its bitterness.

When he'd swallowed it, Bhòid lay back, his eyes unfocused as if he'd partly gone out of himself. Ead called her thrall to hold Bhòid's legs and gave Sulaire a strap to hold his shoulder in place. Sulaire felt sick, but she forced herself to keep the tension on the strap while Ead probed his upper arm with her gnarled fingers, twisted it a little, and started to pull. There was a grating sound, and long before it was over, Bhòid was moaning and couldn't keep back the tears.

When Ead stopped pulling, Bhòid lay as if stunned. Ead wiped the sweat from her face and arms and patted his good shoulder. 'Braver than many a Hunter,' she said, almost regretfully. 'I've done what I can, but it may still heal a little short.'

She turned to Sulaire. 'Kolnos didn't teach you how to do first care for a break like this.'

Sulaire smiled faintly. 'My hands seemed to feel what to do.'

'You didn't flinch when we had to hurt your brother?'

'I had to help. I wanted to learn.'

Ead nodded. 'If you work for me, you will learn.'

Sulaire bowed her head. 'Thank you, Teacher.'

'You will come to the Gathering with me. For now, bind up your brother's arm. Just as you did before.'

A few evenings later, as Sulaire came back towards the village with a basket of yellow woodruff for Ead, she came upon Bhòid kneeling beside a small stack of fallen branches, trying awkwardly to bind them with one hand. Squatting beside him, she tied the knot, keeping her eyes down, unwilling to meet his. With a pang, she realised that she'd been keeping herself apart from him deliberately, because she couldn't bear him to be so unhappy.

'You're learning so much,' he said, and she heard the sullenness in his voice.

'It's not as exciting as I thought. A lot of it is finding the herbs to treat boils and warts, or to make the dye to hide the grey roots of Cosanta's hair.' He grunted and she cast about for something to lessen the distance that seemed to have opened between them. 'You know, Bhòid, I think Ead isn't much of a healer really. Oh yes, warts and boils and a broken bone or a poultice. Things you can learn from watching others. But quite often, she seems almost afraid when I bring back a flower or a root she doesn't know. She's just a small-time village Wise Woman. I don't think she has a nose for it.'

'And you do?'

'An eye and a nose and an ear and a tongue and a tingle in my fingers.'

He gave a half-laugh and she looked at his face. He dashed a tear away with his good hand. 'The Gathering,' he gulped. 'You'll go to the Gathering soon and learn from the great Healers. You'll be away for three moons—more.'

'I must go.'

'I know,' Bhòid said. 'You'll become a Healer. You have the gift. And I will always be a thrall.'

Sulaire looked into his eyes, blue-grey as harebells and wet with tears. Time stopped. She felt a little dizzy, the silence pierced by the distant piping of oystercatchers over the estuary. Behind his tears, deep in the centre of him, lay strength, courage—years stretching before him, years in a place she'd never seen. 'No,' she said slowly. 'You won't always be a thrall.'

'How do you know?'

'I don't *know*. It's as if—as if I *see*. Not with my eyes. In my head.'

He stared at her in the dusk. 'Have you the Sight?' he gasped. 'The Sight as well as the Healing?'

She felt the skin on her face tighten and turn pale. 'Perhaps. It feels—heavy—dangerous. It comes at a cost.' She reached for his hand and held it. Suddenly she longed for the old days, when they were children together and none of these changes were coming between them—as if when Seren and Speir grew up, they had to live one on either side of the Sky River.

As Sulaire trudged along the path between the hills, her pack holding Ead's potions carefully rolled inside a bundle of furs for trading grew heavier. Ead herself had travelled in one of the boats with Fiada and the other Great Ones. If the tides and wind had favoured them, the boats would have reached the Gathering already.

Despite her weariness after yesterday's march, Sulaire looked about her in wonder. On her left, to the north, on the warm south-facing slopes, the woodland was wide and open where the Falcon Clan burned it every dry summer to make the hunting easier. On her right, the forest crawled dark and cold down the north-facing slope, thicker than it grew anywhere near the Beaver village. The old people would say it was full of ghosts, but, for her, this damp forest where the sun never shone was full of new plants and scents. Several times she dropped hastily to her knees to gather an unknown fungus or moss, tucking it into her foraging pouch, scrambling to her feet again before the Hunters who brought up the rear of the band could flick her with their whips.

Ahead of her, Athru and Lufar, with not much more to carry than their sleeping hides and spears, kept pace with the leading Hunters. Sulaire watched their backs, how they walked a little stiff-legged, conscious of their rank, impatient to start Hound training with the youngsters—*the Hunter-caste youngsters*—of all the other Clans of the Bear Tribe.

At midday, the leaders came to a halt at the bottom of a steep pinch, and Sulaire, staggering a little under the weight of her pack, slithered down the slope after them and sat down heavily on the edge of the group, right next to Lufar. As she fell, her pack twisted from her grasp, spilling some its contents. Lufar shrugged and turned away, leaving Sulaire to gather up her scattered load while Athru watched, grinning. Sulaire expected no more of Athru, but she was sorry about Lufar. It was as if the three-year friendship of Cub training had never been. Lufar would follow the path of the Hunter-caste—Hound training, and then, at fifteen summers, when the boys took their Manhood, Lufar would observe the Women's Rites, and some young Hunter from another clan would be made handfast with her.

Sulaire found herself twisting a piece of grass between her hands. Her own path was not so clear. Could a thrall-caste girl ever really become a Healer? Her fingers tore at the grass and she knew, with sudden certainty, how much she wanted more than Ead could ever teach her. She wanted to be more than the Wise Woman of a small clan, conducting the lesser rituals and healing what hurts she could. If she came to a point where she knew she could never be a true Healer—one that the very flowers and roots and leaves told their secrets to—then a light would die in her. For the first time, she really knew how it might feel for Bhòid to think he could never be a Hunter, how lonely he must be in his thralldom.

As the Hunters got lazily to their feet after the rest break and the band set out again, Sulaire followed, unable to get Bhòid out of her mind. Would his arm mend true, or would that be something else for him to bear?

Her pack seemed heavier than this morning, and still the trail led east. At last, when she could barely see for weariness, the trail turned southwards and the burn beside it widened. Sulaire's nose quivered at the salt smell of the estuary borne on the breeze. A little further on, the valley opened before them. She could see the winding water of the Bradan, the river where salmon and sea trout came to spawn, and where the clans gathered every summer for the Salmon Run.

In a curve of the river lay the wide space of the meeting-place of the Bear Tribe—the great council fire in the centre. Around the edge were the clumped huts of the Salmon village, and on the higher side, two buildings greater than any she had seen before. The big house with its thatched roof and south-facing porch nearest the fire—that must be the house of Mathan, Headman of the Salmon Clan, Chieftain of the Bear Tribe. The smaller house, nearer the river, with four tall, white birch poles guarding it—that would be the Moon-house of Sagart, High Priestess of the Moon Goddess.

Below the large village of the Salmon Clan, first clan of the Tribe, lay the summer camp, and beside it a great open space which thrummed with movement as the thralls raised great racks over the smoking fires. A little further on, up a stream that poured fresh water into the brackish tidal reach of the Bradan, was a large hall, thatched, but with open sides, filled with rough tables and benches—the healing hall.

As the rest of the Beavers took the last slope down to the meeting-place almost at a run, Sulaire held back. She thought she could make out Ead's figure standing outside the Moon-house, head bent as if listening to the tall woman beside her who must be Sagart herself.

As Sulaire looked, an old woman came out of the healing hall, wiping her hands on her filthy apron. She stood with her hands on hips, easing her back after the day's work, and then her gaze shifted, up-hill, towards Sulaire, almost as if she'd been waiting for her, and Sulaire knew that she was looking at Oran, the greatest Healer of the Bear Tribe.

Hardly daring to believe that it was herself that Oran was waiting for, Sulaire moved slowly towards the hall. As she drew closer, Sulaire could see the expression on the old woman's face. She looked as if she was tired with all the pain she had seen—and yet her face was filled with warmth, her eyes sparkled and there was humour in her wide mouth.

Before Sulaire had time to drop her pack and kneel respectfully, Oran reached out a hand to stop her. 'The twin,' she said.

'Did Ead …?' asked Sulaire, startled.

'No, child,' answered Oran. 'Ead said nothing of you.' She grunted. 'Hardly seen the woman. She's too busy making up to Sagart.'

'Then how?'

'I have seen you and your brother for many years. I knew one day you would come. I see things. Don't you?'

Her eyes bored into Sulaire.

'Yes,' said Sulaire.

'Don't be afraid,' Oran said, and a light shone in the depth of her dark eyes. 'It is fearsome, but don't be afraid.'

5

UPSETTING THE BALANCE

THE EARLY SUN was shining on the wet mud-flats when Bhòid waded across them and into the estuary. *Swim as much as you can,* Sulaire had said. Day after day he'd pushed himself a little further and today he swam right across the estuary, almost up to the dark edge of the forest that spilled down the slope. Treading water, he stared into the unburned forest no one ever entered, full of bears and wolves, then turned and swam back, floundering across the muddy flat, shaking the water from his hair like a dog, whirling his arms to warm himself, his right arm swinging stiffer and shorter than his left.

Two moons after Sulaire had gone, when their mother cut through the strapping round Bhòid's arm, it had the sweet stink of skin that hasn't had air or water on it for many days. It hung loose, heavy, sore.

When it felt a little stronger, he'd tried casting his throw-spear, but his arm hurt, his balance was out, and the spear flew wide every time. His arm had healed short as Ead had said. He'd tried casting left-handed until his arm ached, but his aim was just as bad. But when he took his sling in his right hand and swung the stone cautiously, keeping the motion mainly in the wrist, it was possible. He'd always been good with the sling. Every day, he worked at it until he found again the speed and snap of the wrist, the eye and timing.

Now he could kill a mountain-hare or a partridge with a single stone. Today, he must bring down something good—if he was lucky, a small buck-fawn, just old enough to leave its mother. Last night, Fiada had returned in the boats, and today Sulaire would return with the overland party.

The light was strong now, and he must be away up the glen before the overseers set him to some other task. Taking his spear and forage-basket, he ran up the hill, skirting the village, making for the point where the Eastern Trail turned the last corner through the autumn woods before coming down the glen. There was no movement on the trail now, but this was the way Sulaire would come.

All morning, he scouted in the woods near the trail, filling his basket with blackberries and fluted-orange mushrooms. As he moved a little further along the trail, he heard a crackling in the undergrowth. Fitting a stone to his sling he waited in the shadows. A capercaillie. An easy target. His stone flew true and the bird fell in a flurry of feathers. It would take a lot of cooking, but tonight it would flavour the broth and tomorrow the meat might be tender enough to chew.

Leaving the bird and his basket under a tree, he gathered fallen branches and stacked them for collecting later—anything to justify staying up here where he could watch the trail. At last, as the sun was streaming through the leaves, he saw the movement of people. He waited, hidden in the birches, suddenly shy. *What if the summer had changed Sulaire? What if she'd gone too far ahead for him to follow?*

Below him Athru and Lufar passed, walking with the Hunters at the head of the line, then the thralls, strung out, travelling slowly under their loads. Even from here he caught the smell of smoked fish. Then Sulaire came round the bend, and although she couldn't possibly have seen him from the trail, she glanced towards where he stood and her eyes shone with knowing he was there. Bhòid scuttered down the bank towards her, dropping his spear, basket and bird at her feet.

She felt up and down his broken arm. 'It's healed well,' she said. 'You've grown. You're nearly as tall as me.'

He could tell from her eyes that she'd grown in more than height. She'd seen things, learned things and she seemed years older now than he was. A sense of loss washed over him, and before he could stop himself he muttered, 'You smell of fish.'

'Of course I do,' she answered crossly. 'What do you expect when I've carried Ead's winter supply for two days?'

He looked again and saw that she was dog-weary. 'I'm sorry,' he said. "Give me your pack; you take the bird and the basket.'

Wrangling the heavy pack onto his shoulders, he asked, 'How did you carry it so far? All day? All day yesterday?' She shrugged. He saw a shadow cross her face. 'Sulaire? What happened?'

She paused, as if it was hard to put into words. Then she stretched out her hand, tentatively, and touched the nick on his shoulder, the nick she'd made when they asked the gods for totems. 'Oran,' she said. 'Oran welcomed me. She knew about you. She can see things. She taught me. I learned more than I ever thought possible. And Ead is jealous.'

As their eyes met, he seemed to see all that she'd felt—the learning, the comfort of Oran, the enmity of Ead. He put his hand over hers. 'Will Ead still let you work for her?'

'Oh yes,' Sulaire said. 'She's getting old and stiff. I can gather plants she can't reach herself. I know what to gather when her thrall doesn't. I can carry whatever she gives me to carry. I can be useful. Especially now, when winter's coming.'

The water was still cold, but the spring sun was warm on Bhòid's back, and for now at least, hauling armfuls of seaweed from beside the breakwater, with Sulaire working on the beach nearby, he felt happy.

All through late autumn and winter, Ead had kept Sulaire busy doing the filthiest tasks that went with healing. She'd sent her out in harsh weather, scouring the hills for red lingonberries, mouse-ear for coughs and burdock for cleansing the blood. But even if Ead worked her like a thrall, Sulaire was learning. Bhòid saw the growing confidence in her hands as she massaged their mother's chest, the eagerness with which she tried new herbs to ease the coughing. She was learning more every day, while he was stuck with the endless chores of fetching water and firewood and cleaning hides.

Sometimes the years seemed to stretch before him, grey in their sameness. Their fourteenth summer was coming. They were nearly grown up. In a year or two maybe Sulaire wouldn't return from the Gathering. She'd become Oran's apprentice, or another clan might ask for her, and she'd go, perhaps across water, perhaps far to the north, and he'd never see her again. He pushed the thought away. Today the seaweed harvest was good and the sun was warm. Today he'd be happy.

He gathered up a bundle of kelp and laver and carried it to the drying racks where Sulaire was sorting the weed for Ead—some good for stiff joints, some for belly-ache. Ead herself was dozing on a rock in the sun nearby, and wouldn't notice if he paused for a few words with Sulaire. As he stood beside her a flight of swifts—the first this year—came screaming overhead. Sulaire looked up, and together they watched the birds spin over the water.

'Where do they come from?' he asked.

'Somewhere else,' she said, smiling.

Bhòid would have stayed a little longer watching the swifts wheel and rise, but Ead shifted on her rock and half opened her eyes. Running back down to the sea before he could get Sulaire into trouble, he waded back into the waves beside the breakwater that formed a fish trap at the end of the beach.

On the trap side, Athru and Lufar, waist-deep in the sheltered water, were vying with each other to spear the biggest fish while Fiada stood on the rocks of the breakwater, shouting encouragement.

Further along the breakwater, a few children, three or four summers old, moved along the rocks collecting periwinkles, a small boy farther out than the rest, almost at the end. As Bhòid watched, a wave washed over the rocks and knocked the boy into the open water on Bhòid's side of the breakwater. The next wave sucked him out as the other children watched in horror. Before anyone else could move, Bhòid plunged deeper into the water, half-wading, half-swimming. With the tide running out, he thought he might never reach the boy, that he himself might be washed away, but an incoming wave brought the boy a little nearer and Bhòid grabbed a handful of his hair. Struggling to keep his footing and drag the child to the shore, Bhòid was suddenly aware of Fiada threshing towards him, reaching a strong arm to pull him in.

As his feet found their grip on the sand, Bhòid clutched the child, Parsa, to his chest. His lips were blue, his eyes closed. He felt cool in Bhòid's arms. He had no breath. Bhòid couldn't bear the boy to be dead. 'Parsa,' he called as he ran, 'Parsa, come back.'

He ran towards Ead—she'd know what to do—but when he reached her, the old woman merely glanced at the inert figure in his arms and shrugged. 'He's dead,' Ead said, and turned her head away as if the death of the boy—just a thrall—was of no importance.

Willing his warmth into the limp body, Bhòid turned to Sulaire. 'Hold him by the feet,' she said.

Bhòid quickly tipped the child upside down while Sulaire slapped his back until a gush of water came out of his mouth. Bhòid swung him upright again, but still he didn't breathe.

Sulaire took the child in her arms, raised her eyes to the sky, and knelt on the sand. 'He has lost his breath,' she said. 'I must lend him some of mine.' She put her mouth to the pale lips, blew, turned her head, breathed in, and blew again. Breathed and blew, breathed and blew, until, with a fluttering tremor, the child's chest lifted. Parsa coughed, drew a breath, and started to cry.

Bhòid took the child and held him, feeling the shuddering sobs against his chest and a flooding sense of happiness that the boy was alive.

Only then did he become fully aware of others who'd run to watch.

Athru glaring at him with the old hatred.

Parsa's mother, who'd been standing as if frozen with terror, bursting forward, snatching the boy from his arms, staring wildly at Bhòid as if he was the danger.

Fiada looking from Sulaire to Bhòid to Ead, asking, 'Is this a sign from the gods? That she made the child alive again when even you could not?'

Ead hissing, 'A sign? A sign to fear! She, a thrall, usurping the power of the Goddess! Upsetting the Balance, reversing death! Pray that the harm falls on her, not on the Clan!'

The bystanders flinching from the curse and drifting away; Fiada, his eyes full of trouble, following them.

Ead dismissing Sulaire with a bitter gesture, and a single word, 'Go!'

Sulaire, sinking back on the sand, pale, almost shrunken, as if the healing—and Ead's curse—had taken some of her own life from her.

6

GANNETS DIVING

THE SUN WAS setting as Bhòid came through the village, a basket of mussels and sea lettuce under one arm, striding straight ahead, ignoring the women who hurried inside in case his shadow fell on them. The overseers were the same, he thought, always setting him and Sulaire at tasks that kept them a distance from everyone else. Even Fiada couldn't look at him, and Athru would turn away with a sneer and a flick of his plaits. Everyone seemed afraid of the twins. But when Bhòid passed Ead's house and saw the icy look she cast him, he thought *No, it's Ead they're afraid of. And with Athru it's jealousy.*

Outside one of the huts, Parsa was playing with a couple of sticks. His face lit up when he saw Bhòid, and he ran towards him, but before the boy could reach him, his mother called to him harshly. Parsa stopped where he was, looking up at Bhòid with bright dark eyes. Then his mother shouted again, and he went to her, dragging his feet.

When Bhòid ducked into the hut, Sulaire sat huddled by the meagre fire, looking pinched with cold despite the warmth of early summer. She was stirring listlessly at a pot that held little but mallow roots. Now that she was nothing more than a thrall, Bhòid thought, now that the villagers were afraid of her, she seemed to have lost her sense of herself, as if Ead's anger was seeping into her bones like a slow poison.

'She's going to the Gathering tomorrow,' he said. 'It will be easier when she's gone.'

Sulaire shook her head. 'Maybe I'll never see Oran again.'

'Nonsense,' he said firmly. 'Of course you will.' He added the mussels and greens to the pot, stirred a little to heat them through, and passed Sulaire a bowlful. 'Try, Sulaire. You'll feel better when you've eaten this. Besides, Mother needs her massage.'

'Even she's afraid of us now.' Sulaire's voice was bleak. 'Everyone's afraid of us. They think we're touched by the gods, but we're only thralls. They wonder what we'll do next, and whether we *have* upset the Balance.

Charlotte Clutterbuck

'Nonsense,' he said again. 'It's Ead they're afraid of. And Balance or no, Mother feels better when you massage her.'

Almost as soon as Fiada and his household had left for the Gathering, Ead with them, Sulaire lost her pinched look. One day Bhòid came back to the village to find that she was up on one of the roofs, helping old Thorn, who'd always been fond of her, to mend the thatch. They were laughing together, and when they'd finished, Sulaire dropped lightly down from the roof. As Thorn followed in his turn, he stumbled a little, and Sulaire looked at him sharply.

'It's my ankle,' he said, 'it catches me after a day on the roof.'

'Sit down,' said Sulaire, and the old man sat on a nearby log. Sulaire knelt at his feet, fishing a small horn of ointment from her pouch, and Bhòid stayed to watch his sister as she stroked and massaged Thorn's ankle. How intent she was, how deft her hands were. A little more colour came into Thorn's face, and when she'd finished and gestured to him to stand, he bent and kissed her swiftly on the cheek. Only then did Bhòid

74

notice that a few villagers had drifted up to watch from a safe distance.

After that, the thralls started to come shyly to Sulaire with their hurts and illnesses. They took the potions she offered for a sore tooth or let her dress a festering oyster-gash, and then scurried away, leaving small gifts of food or wood.

Bhòid saw that she'd found her way again.

The summer moons passed, warm and dry. The heather was in bloom and the twins spent days ranging the purple slopes above the village plucking heather for the thrall women to make beer. One evening in very early autumn, as they came down to the estuary to wash away the day's sun and sweat, Bhòid saw, dark against the sunset, a flock of gannets diving for fish. Hundreds of birds spearing out of the air faster than the eye could follow, the water spurting from the gilded waves as they plunged beneath the surface.

He watched Sulaire stand on the shore, a contained energy quivering through her whole body, her eyes lit with the glow of late sun on water. She raised her arms like an ascending bird, ducked and dived, leaped across the sand—a mirror dance to the wild sky-dance of the birds.

He stood transfixed.

Then the sun dipped behind the distant hills and the gannets were gone.

Something in Sulaire was changed, something in her eyes, the way she held herself, balanced somewhere between awe and joy, and Bhòid saw that she and her totem had found each other.

'Did you know?' he whispered, remembering that day in their ninth year when a great bird's wings had seemed to beat above their heads. 'You're named for the Gannet.'

'I always hoped. This time, I knew. The Gannets chose me.'

He felt suddenly bereft, as if once more she'd gone far beyond him. His heart clamoured to know if there was no totem for him, if a thrall could truly not have a totem, but he didn't want to taint her moment. As if she knew how he felt, Sulaire took his hand and they walked home in silence.

A few days later Bhòid came in after a day spent helping to dig foundations for a new store-shed.

He tossed a bundle of firewood roughly down by the fire and broke their mother's best clay pot.

'Clumsy, clumsy, clumsy,' she snapped.

'After all I do!' he snapped back and blundered out of the hut.

When Sulaire joined him on the training ground, he was casting sling-stones with vicious speed, missing more often than he hit the target. He glared at her, but she reached out to touch his arm.

'Yours will come.'

'When? When?'

She shook her head. 'That's not for me to say.'

'And what? What totem will choose me now?'

She took him by the ears, half laughing, half serious. 'A squirrel, as I said when we were children. Feorag—a bright, bouncy, greedy, fiery little squirrel who knows how to look after its young.'

'Only the females do that,' he scoffed. 'I'm not a girl.'

'Totem isn't male or female,' she said. 'Totem is above male and female, above big and small, above high and low.' She poked him in the ribs. 'For all we know, Snail could be Totem. Or Dormouse—they're great nibblers.'

He looked at her, shocked. 'Snail! Dormouse! Don't jest, Sulaire. Don't mock the gods.'

'I'm not mocking,' she said, with the glimmer of a smile, 'but I think the gods must have a sense of humour, or they'd be less than us, not more.'

That year the Beavers who'd gone to the Gathering brought back more than dried salmon and flint knives. Soon after their return one of the youngest thralls fell ill with a terrible fever—something even Ead hadn't seen before. Within days, many followed and Bhòid saw Ead prowling the village, keeping her distance as her thrall went to each hut looking for early signs of the illness. He carried the sick, mostly children, to a hut outside the village. Every morning he placed food and water at the door. Those strong enough to crawl could eat and drink and might recover.

Each morning on his way to work, Bhòid saw the thralls carrying those who had died in the night up the hill to bury them. Without the children, the village was silent. Those who were well went sullenly about their work—so much more work to do with fewer hands—and Bhòid was busy from dawn till dusk.

A few days after the illness came, Bhòid had just come out of a store-hut after emptying a load of hazelnuts when he saw Ead standing a short distance from his own hut. He raced across the meeting-place in time to see her thrall stooped at the narrow doorway, lifting Sulaire over his shoulder. Sulaire's eyes were open but seemed to see nothing. His heart lurched in his chest. If he let the thrall take her to the sick-hut, she'd die.

'You can't take her,' Bhòid cried, rushing at the thrall, but the man flung Bhòid to the ground with his free arm.

'She has the fever,' Ead said curtly, withering Bhòid with a look of triumph as she turned back into the village, leaving the thrall to carry Sulaire away.

Bhòid leaped up and took his mother's arm. 'Stop them,' he shouted. 'She'll die!'

His mother shook her head helplessly. 'It happened so suddenly. She couldn't get up this morning. And then the thrall came.' She brushed away a tear. 'What could I do?'

Bhòid stared at her, stunned. Then he dived into the hut and flung an old deerskin onto the floor.

'What are you doing?' cried his mother.

'Getting ready to fetch Sulaire,' he snapped, reaching into the rafters for a length of rope. His mother tried to hold him back, but he pushed her aside, snarling. She snatched his hair in both hands and forced him to look at her.

'Better that one should live!' she cried.

He looked back at her with a cold fierceness he'd never felt before, broke away and finished collecting dried meat, leather rags, rope and gut, a few tools, a rough clay pot with a piece of smouldering tinder fungus in it and another of seal fat.

When he'd bundled everything together he crouched in the doorway, peering out. Ead was at the far end of the village. He waited until her back was turned, then snatched up his bundle and dashed behind the nearest hut. Slinking from hut to hut, he crept out of the village, into the woods and up a side-stream close to the burial ground—a spot the Clan avoided for fear of the dead. Leaving his bundle in a grassy dell, praying that he wasn't too late, he ran back down the hill towards the sick-hut.

Holding his breath against the stench and muck inside the hut, he stepped over two children—one crying weakly, one lying still. When he bent over

Sulaire, she put her arms round his neck. Like everything in the hut, she was filthy. He hauled her onto his back and left the hut, staggering under her weight, but doggedly plodding on until he'd reached the spot he'd chosen.

Laying Sulaire on the grass, he stripped off her filthy tunic and his own and cleaned himself and the clothes in the running water. Then he wet rags to wash his sister. She was burning hot and her breath fluttered and rasped. When she was clean, he laid her on one of the damp tunics and put the other over her to cool her, but it all had to be done again when she suddenly vomited.

As soon as she was clean again and quiet, he searched for bog myrtle leaves, smearing the juice on their skin to keep off the clouds of midges that whined round them.

'There must be medicine,' he said, begging her, but Sulaire just stared at him with glazed eyes.

Leaving her, he ran back to the village, and found Ead walking across the meeting-place. She looked at him coldly, but he forced back the surge of fear in his throat. 'Medicine,' he gasped, 'I need medicine.'

Ead laughed harshly. 'If you've taken her from the sick-hut, you may well die with her. There's no medicine for this.' She spat on the ground and turned away.

Bhòid stood alone in the centre of the village—deserted as if everyone was away or hiding. Then he saw his mother standing at the door of their hut, holding a small horn at arm's length, as if she was frightened to touch him. 'Honey, with heather,' she said. 'Sulaire made it for my chest. Maybe it will help.'

He snatched the horn and raced back up the hill. Sulaire was tossing feverishly and already the evening breeze was riffling through the leaves. By morning it would be cold and the dew would wet her. Choosing a spot where a hazel was sprouting near a bare patch of grass, he bound the tips of several saplings together with gut, then used the rope to pull them towards the earth and tied them to the base of a nearby tree so that their curve formed the shape of a tent.

Making a small fireplace of stones near the mouth of the tent, he gathered sticks and lichen and blew on the tinder fungus until small flames licked at the kindling. Then he fetched water in the pot, wedged it among the stones, and built up the fire round it.

While the water was heating, he flung an old hide over the saplings, lashing it down as best he could. Then he lifted Sulaire into the tent, laid her on his tunic, and poured a little of the medicine into the hot water. She lay there, struggling to breathe as he spooned some of the heather tea into her. Her breathing calmed a little and she fell into a fitful sleep.

Food tasted like bark in his mouth, but Bhòid forced himself to chew on some dried meat. Then he lay on the grass near Sulaire and slept. Every time she moaned or shifted in her sleep, he jerked awake and gave her more tea.

For four days he tended her, washing her, heating tea and making broth with dried meat and sorrel. She could drink the tea, but mostly the broth made her vomit.

On the fifth morning, when he raised her against his shoulder to hold the horn of tea to her mouth, he could feel the bones in her back, and there was no strength in any of her limbs. That afternoon a storm broke with a piercing rain that swept through their scanty shelter, drenching Sulaire. When the storm ceased, he spread out the bedding to dry, but at nightfall everything was still damp.

In the early morning, her voice woke him. She was shaking with fever, her skin dry, her lips cracked, her eyes dull. All day she thrashed and muttered, and towards evening she gave a loud shriek and wailed something about the Moon Goddess. He thought that she didn't know him, but when he drew closer, her eyes cleared for a moment and her lips moved. 'Mistletoe … ivy-leaves … tea.'

He found the ivy and mistletoe on a great oak a little way into the wood, but when he returned with them, he had no idea how many leaves to use, or in how much water. Sulaire was drenched in sweat, her lips covered in white foam.

'Gannet Spirit,' he prayed, tossing a handful of leaves into the pot, 'Moon, Seren and Speir, help us.' When the tea was cool enough, he helped her drink, but the fever raged on, and she raved, wild-eyed, while he sponged her and felt the life seeping out of her.

At last she quietened a little and he fell beside her, exhausted, and slept. At first light he woke. She lay motionless, so cool that he cried out, thinking she was dead. Then her eyelids fluttered open. She looked at him, knowing him, and he knew that the fever had gone.

Before he could stop himself, he was sobbing and howling with relief. She weakly raised her right hand to stroke his head before falling into a deep sleep.

Still hiccupping and sobbing, he left her sleeping and went fishing. He caught two trout and laid the best on a stone by the oak to thank the gods. The other, he made into broth. This time Sulaire drank it gratefully and slept again.

Next morning, she tried to sit up, but when he went to help her, she looked at him, terrified.

'My leg!' she cried.

Bhòid stared, appalled, at her left leg, lying limp and useless.

'I'll never be a Healer now,' she wailed. 'A cripple can't be a Healer. I can't even walk.'

'You'll walk,' he said. 'You'll know what to do, even if Ead won't help.'

She shook her head. Looking at her white face, he understood. Her power didn't tell her how to heal herself. Not now, in the terror of being suddenly crippled.

'Lie on your front,' he said and set himself to massaging her leg with seal fat. At first he was clumsy and uncertain, but after a little while he got the feel for it, the rhythm, letting the shape and give in her leg tell his hands what to do. Then he soaked the hides in the hot water he always kept near the fire, and wrapped her leg.

He scoured the forest until he found two fallen branches with the shape he wanted—long shafts, with the stump of a thicker branch at the top. With his knife, he carved the shafts to the same length, then scraped the stumps smooth, padding them with hide. He chose two stout sticks for splints and trimmed them to the length of her leg.

It took him all day. When he'd finished, he bound the splints to her left leg and then helped her to stand so that the crutches took most of her weight as she moved, good foot, bad foot, good foot. By then, she was moaning with the pain and concentration of movement.

'Three steps,' he said, 'tomorrow, ten.'

Leaving the crutches, he took her on his back and carried her down the glen a little way to a slab of rock that looked out over the estuary. For a long time, they sat looking over the empty water.

As the light faded, a single gannet appeared, hovering and diving far out over the water.

7

FEORAG

ICICLES DRIPPED FROM the thatch as Sulaire crawled outside the hut to bring in a little more firewood from the pile stacked by the wall. If only she were strong enough to do more to help her brother through this bitter winter. With only Bhòid to do the family's thrall-work and gather food and firewood for them all, the hut was never really warm and there was never quite enough to eat. She knew he took less than his share of the food. He'd grown taller, and he was so thin. Each morning, he'd be up long before first light, setting water to heat, kneeling beside Sulaire, rubbing her leg and foot with hands that had become deft and confident. Then he'd help her to walk, a few steps further than the day before. When she lay down to rest, he'd use the hot water to make a compress for her leg. And when the sky was just beginning to lighten, he'd set out for a full day's thrall-work with almost nothing in his belly, while all day their mother sat hunched by the fire and coughed.

But this morning, Bhòid was still sleeping, and Sulaire felt good to be the one working. When she'd brought in some wood to warm by the fire, she crawled out again, broke off some icicles, and left them to thaw in a pot inside the door. Then she poked up the fire and threw some herbs into the clay pot they used for making tea.

When the tea was ready, she dipped out a cupful. As she crawled to where their mother slept in the warmest spot against the wall, Sulaire suddenly stopped. There was something wrong in the way her mother lay in a tumbled heap. There was no sound of rasping breath. Sulaire felt the keening start in her throat.

'Sulaire?' Bhòid's voice was thick with sleep.

'Mother,' cried Sulaire, 'Mother is dead.'

Bhòid groped his way from his side of the fire, put one arm round Sulaire, and laid his free hand on their mother's body. He sighed, but said nothing.

Sulaire laid her head on his shoulder and felt the tears well up in her eyes.

'She can rest now, Sulaire. At least she can rest now.' Sulaire felt his arms tighten round her, and a shudder in his chest. 'It's just the two of us now,' he said.

Shaking himself, he got up and set about stretching and lashing the thin hide he wore as a cloak over two hazel-rods to make a travois. Her brother looked almost numb with weariness as he eased their mother's stick-thin body onto the hide sling and dragged it towards the space on the hill where the thralls always buried their dead. His back was bowed and he limped as if the stones on the path were cutting through his worn-out shoes. As she watched her mother's last pitiful journey, Sulaire went on keening for the woman who'd lived her whole life bound to the village, with nothing beyond and little joy.

When he came back to fetch Sulaire, Bhòid's fingers were knife-points of cold as he took her hands. He helped her onto his back and carried her to the place where he and the other thralls had scraped a shallow trench.

As Bhòid and the thralls laid her mother in the soil, Sulaire scattered herbs into the grave and then stood as straight as she could to chant the sacred words:

*A life lived, breath to sky. A life lived, body
to earth. Talamh, earth mother, take this
woman into your lap.*

Her heart ached, but no tears came as Bhòid
took the hide from the travois—the hide that was
all he had by way of a cloak—and laid it over their
mother's body. He scraped the earth over it and
then covered her with stones.

As Bhòid carried Sulaire home, she could feel
how thin he was, how he shivered without his
cloak. There must be something more she could
do to help him, she thought. Even if she'd been
strong enough to forage for healing herbs, there
was little enough to be found in the winter
forest, and no chance that the villagers would
seek her for healing now that the gods' anger
had fallen on her. But there must be something
she could do.

Next day she took their mother's spare tunic
and stitched a patterned border round its neck,
covering the blemishes and patches with swirls
of tiny shells, making it strong again and pretty.
She laid it on a rock just outside the door where
anyone passing would see it. For a few days

nothing happened, but one morning she found a young Hunter standing shyly outside with a fresh hide. He asked her to make a smock for his woman, who was bearing their first child. Soon enough many of the women were bringing her old tunics to mend, paying with dried meat or a fox pelt that she could stich into a hood to trade again.

As the days grew longer, Sulaire could haul herself further on her crutches, and the villagers began to get used to her again and lost some of their fear. Gradually, the thralls who couldn't afford the large gifts Ead expected started to creep back, and Sulaire's hands grew strong and clever on sore shoulders and wrenched ankles. She pounded and steeped herbs for fevers and headaches and sore teeth, and those she helped returned with firewood or a handful of nuts, though they'd also make a quick gesture to ward off the evil spirits.

But if anyone had an evil spirit, Sulaire thought, it was Athru. Tall, with fine-cut, bold features, Athru was good to look at and he knew it—preening and decking his Hunter's plaits with feathers—but he was cruel. Quick to beat a thrall, kick the dogs away from the fire or twist the ears of small children until they cried. Once, when he thought no one was looking, Sulaire saw something else in his green eyes—a dark, hunted look as if he was afraid.

One day, when Athru kicked a crutch from under her, Sulaire fell heavily, and he stepped on her hand before turning away.

Bhòid stood staring after Athru, clenching his fists. 'Be quiet, now,' Sulaire gasped, 'you'll only get yourself a beating.'

'He's cowardly and cruel,' said Bhòid.

Sulaire shook her head, 'He's unhappy and afraid. I don't know why.'

'I don't want him hurting you.'

'Then I must get stronger and better at avoiding him,' she said.

She exchanged her crutches for a staff and each day she walked a little farther, keeping well away from Athru. Her thoughts were harder to avoid. She'd seen hate in Bhòid's eyes as he stood back and let Athru walk away. He wasn't a hater, her brother; he mustn't become a hater. Their fifteenth spring was coming, and after it the Gathering. If Athru came unscathed out of the Boar Hunt and the Man-Making that followed, he'd be a full Hunter of the Bear Tribe and would have even more power over Bhòid. Sometimes Sulaire caught Bhòid looking down the estuary to the hills beyond the loch and knew that he dreamed of escaping. If it had been just him, he might have grown his hair to cover the brand and taken to the trading trails, or become a wild man of the forest, living on his own with the animals, but she knew he would never leave her.

Each night before she slept, she prayed: *Merak, Great Bear, my brother is brave and kind as Speir was. He needs your help.*

The tail-end of winter had brought a run of bright days and Sulaire was in a wooded glade above the village, helping the four-and-five-year-olds grub mallow roots. The wind was cool, but birds were beginning to nest. Across the glade, Bhòid was taking the taller children one by one, boosting them into a tree, showing them how to find an early nest, how to take only one egg and come down without falling and breaking it.

The boy Parsa, none the worse for his near-drowning, was the most agile. For a while Sulaire watched Bhòid climbing a sycamore, hoisting Parsa after him, leading him up towards a cross-bill's nest. A little later, she looked up and saw Bhòid drop from the lowest branch, an egg held gently in one hand. He stowed the egg in his basket and reached up to catch Parsa as he leaped down. She could hear them laughing as they went in search of another nest. A flash of red-gold caught her eye as a squirrel bounded across the grassy glade and scuttered up the trunk in front of the boys. Bhòid paused at the bottom, looking up at the squirrel, and then moved on with Parsa to the next tree, leaving the squirrel cleaning its whiskers undisturbed.

If Bhòid was happy today, Athru wasn't. He leaned against a tree on the other side of the clearing, sullenly watching two young thralls cut hazel rods, whippy with spring sap. He was resentful, Sulaire thought, that instead of hunting boar with the full-grown men, he was left overseeing the thralls. Luckily he seemed to think that Sulaire and the children were beneath his attention, and stayed where he was, fiddling with the binding of his spear.

The earth crumbled between Sulaire's fingers as she pushed her digging stick under the roots.

When the baskets were heavy with roots, Sulaire led the children to a bank of early primroses to fill the last spaces in their baskets with leaves and flowers to add to their supper.

The squirrel's warning squeal slashed through the quiet of the morning. Sulaire jerked herself upright, following the direction of the squirrel's gaze. She heard the snap of a stick as something moved in the forest. She saw Bhòid snatch Parsa up in his arms and race across the clearing towards her, dropping the boy at her feet. As Sulaire gathered all the children to her, the birds fell silent and the cracking of wood in the forest grew louder. Bhòid stepped between Sulaire and the children and whatever was coming out of the trees, fitting a stone to his sling.

When the bear came lumbering into the clearing, time seemed to freeze. Sulaire heard a child wailing. She saw an old bear, toothless, angry after the hard winter, the strength of hunger on it, shaking its head as it looked round the clearing—at Athru, the thralls, Bhòid, Sulaire and the children—making its choice. She saw Athru, his face white with terror; heard him shouting, 'Run!' She saw Athru and the thralls bounding across the clearing and flinging themselves away down the hill as the bear came padding slowly towards her.

Bhòid stood still between her and the bear, bellowing, 'Stand! Make noise! Throw stones, baskets, anything!'

The bear broke into a clumsy trot, flinching at Bhòid's first stone, shaking off the children's shower of pebbles and root-filled baskets. Sulaire heard her own voice yelling, and held her digging stick ready in one hand, staff in the other. She saw the bear's small eyes, its red mouth, smelled the stench of its breath. She heard the whizz of another stone leaving Bhòid's sling, and the bear suddenly stopped, shaking its head. A third stone hit its shoulder and the bear slowly turned and shambled back into the woods.

While Sulaire clutched the smallest children into her arms and calmed their wailing, the bigger ones gathered the scattered roots and flowers. Bhòid crossed the clearing and looked up into the tree where the squirrel still crouched. When Sulaire joined him with the children, Bhòid was standing with his hands raised, the squirrel watching him with its huge dark eyes.

As Bhòid turned to Sulaire, his eyes seemed a deeper blue, as if something had changed in him. 'It wasn't just the warning,' he said, 'I could feel the squirrel giving me courage.'

She nodded 'Merak has shown you your totem.'

'Red Squirrel, *Feorag*,' he said in a shaky voice. '*Feorag*,' he said again, as if testing the squirrel's formal name in his mouth. He took an egg from the basket he'd left lying on the ground, and laid it on the grass under the tree in offering.

'And something for Merak,' he said. He pulled the knife from his belt and hacked away a hank of his hair, laying it on the track where the bear had vanished. He looked up at Sulaire. 'I didn't know Merak was so terrible,' he faltered.

As Bhòid and Sulaire walked down the glen, the children holding fast to their hands, they came on the two thralls, dithering shamefaced, afraid to go back to the village without the children. Athru stood a little apart, with a sick, white look on his face, his mouth open like a beached fish, gasping for breath.

Sulaire felt sorry for him—anyone might run from a bear. Before she could think what to do, how to stop Bhòid from walking so stiffly, pride written in every line of his body, Fiada came down the burn at the head of a band of Hunters, a boar slung between their spears. Fiada paused, looking at the children clinging to Bhòid and Sulaire. His glance shifted, he stared at his son and Athru couldn't meet his father's eyes. Fiada resettled the weight of the boar on his shoulder and moved on.

As the twins passed Athru, Sulaire felt the force of his hatred like the bear's stinking breath, and suddenly her head swam, and she saw, almost as if it was still happening, the Night of the Totems—the dark of the woods, the dim shape of the owl flitting over their heads, the rank smell of the bear, the flash of moonlight on the salmon in its mouth. Then her head cleared and she followed Bhòid down the track.

'Athru ran from his own totem,' he said contemptuously over his shoulder.

'Perhaps not,' Sulaire said slowly. 'Perhaps it's Salmon that's his totem, not Bear. Remember the salmon in the bear's mouth on the night of the totems?'

Bhòid stared back at her. 'But Kolnos …? He wouldn't get something like that wrong?'

'Not everyone has the true power in their hearts. Kolnos and Ead play the role, but their hearts are ruled by something else. Maybe, because Kolnos loves power and knows Athru will be Headman, he gave Athru the wrong totem, and now Merak is angry and has shamed him.'

Bhòid shuddered. 'I feel almost sorry for him'.

'Oh yes,' she said, 'it would be harder to be him than you.'

8

FLIGHT

FOR SEVERAL DAYS, the weather had held warm for early spring. Sweat trickled down Bhòid's chest as he hacked through the tough stems of the bracken with his sickle. He stripped off his jerkin and worked on in his kilt, the small leather bag that hung from his belt bumping at his thigh.

'What's this?' he'd asked, when Sulaire gave him the bag that morning. It was clean, freshly oiled, a small replica of the bag she always carried at her waist. 'What's this?' he asked again. Her grey eyes met his, fathomless, as if she was in some other place. 'Be safe on your journey, Bhòid,' was all she said.

'What journey?' he asked, grasping her shoulder. 'I'm not going anywhere. Not without you.' She shook her head, took her staff, and set off up the hill. Despite her lameness, she moved with a grace of her own.

'Come,' she called over her shoulder, 'There'll be trouble if you're late for work,' and he tied the bag to his belt and followed, wondering.

Now he left the bag hitched to his belt, his sling tucked beside it, and went on sawing at the fronds that would make fresh bedding for the Great Ones. From time to time, he glanced at Sulaire as she crouched alongside him with the other thralls, but she just worked on in silence.

Nearby, a few early bees hummed amongst the blackthorns along the burn. Bhòid could hear Ead's thrall cursing as he reached into the spiny bushes for the blossom while Ead sat in the sun and watched. Further up the slope two young Hunters, today's overseers, sat furbishing their spears, their hounds lying at their feet. They took scant notice of the thralls, merely glancing down the hill every so often to see if anyone was slacking.

All morning Bhòid worked his way across the slope, leaving piles of bracken in his wake. Around midday the wind swung round to the north, and the clouds thickened. The thralls started binding the bracken into bundles and stacking them on the bank above the burn. As Bhòid squatted to tighten a rope, the wind cold now on his bare back, someone spoke near him. 'A mighty Hunter,' the voice said, sneering, and a ripple of suppressed laughter ran amongst the thralls.

Bhòid lifted his head to see what they were laughing at, and saw Athru coming down the hill with a mountain hare dangling from one fist. 'A very mighty Hunter,' came another voice, and Bhòid knew that the thralls had heard the story of how Athru had run from the bear.

Athru knew it too. As he neared the burn, he glanced around the group of thralls, and at Ead, coming down the burn. Tossing his hare to the ground, he drew himself up to his full height, glowering.

'This summer,' he said loudly, thrusting out his chin and tapping his spear against his calf, 'This summer at the Gathering, I will be made a Man of the Bear Tribe. Then we will see.' As his eyes swept from one thrall to another, the smirks faded from their faces and the two who'd run with him from the bear hung their heads.

Then his gaze shifted to Bhòid, his hand tightening on his spear, raising the point. Bhòid braced himself for the attack, but even Athru could hardly kill him in front of everyone. Something flickered in Athru's green eyes—a new thought. Thrusting his spear into the earth at Bhòid's feet where it quivered like a threat, he shrugged contemptuously, and swung round to where Sulaire was bent over a bundle of bracken, watching.

Athru moved steadily towards her. 'And after the Man-Making,' he said slowly, as if thinking it out, 'at the Dance of Increase, I will choose the fairest of the young women.' He looked down at Sulaire as if he'd never really seen her before. 'Your face is not bad to look at, Sulaire,' he went on, 'but I think I will choose a fairer woman from the greatest Clan—Salmon perhaps—to come back with me as my woman.'

Sulaire looked down, twisting a piece of rope between her fingers.

'Stand when I'm speaking to you,' Athru said, with a quiet menace.

Watching Sulaire get stiffly to her feet, Bhòid felt a chill that was more than the north wind on his back. He raised himself from a squat to a crouch, but Sulaire shot a warning glance at him, and he froze, tense and ready.

'And when I bring this fairest of women home and build my own house,' Athru continued slowly, 'I think I will take you as second woman, Sulaire.' He turned to Ead. 'Once I am a man, I will have the right to my handfast-woman and a second woman if I want, won't I, Wise Woman?'

'Certainly,' said Ead, looking down at Sulaire with something like triumph in her eyes, 'as one who will be Headman, you may take a second woman if you wish.'

'Well, Sulaire,' said Athru, 'what do you say? It is a great thing for a thrall to be second woman to a Headman.'

Sulaire raised her eyes to Athru's. 'I will be a Healer,' she said quietly.

'A Healer!' Athru scoffed, 'with your crippled leg? Tell her, Ead, a cripple cannot be a Healer.'

'The Moon Goddess calls only those who are perfect,' Ead replied.

Sulaire looked levelly at Athru. 'Nonetheless the Goddess has called me. I am a Healer.'

Athru pulled Sulaire towards him roughly. 'Not if your face is scarred.' In a flash he had his knife out, his fist raised. Quick as thought, Bhòid launched himself forward, arm outstretched, forcing Athru's hand downwards so that the knife slashed Sulaire's forearm instead of her face.

Knocking Bhòid aside with a swipe of his arm, Athru raised the knife again towards Sulaire's face. Bhòid gave a sudden roar of rage, and Athru, startled, hesitated for a fraction of time, long enough for Bhòid to lower his head and charge. He butted Athru in the belly, sending the knife flying. Athru crashed back down the bank, cracking his head against a rock, lying white-faced, half in the stream, blood oozing from his scalp.

Before Bhòid could move, Sulaire had dropped on her knees beside Athru, laying her palm over the wound. Ead shambled towards them, shrieking, and from the corner of his eye Bhòid saw the two Hunters starting down the hill to see what the trouble was.

Bhòid looked down at Sulaire, at the blood trickling from the gash in her arm.

'Go,' she said fiercely. 'He'll live, I'll live, but they'll kill you. Go!'

He stretched his hand towards her, but already the Hunters were running down the hill, their hounds leaping beside them.

'What use are you to me if you're dead?' Sulaire cried. 'I *will* live. Run! Now!'

Her certainty thrust him into movement. Clambering up the bank, he snatched up his sickle and ran. From the corner of his eye, he saw some of the thralls joining the chase.

Southwards and down he ran, towards the estuary, the bag Sulaire had given him thumping against his flank, the clamour of men and dogs and Ead's shrill cries behind him. He could almost smell the blood-lust of the chase—if they caught him, they'd kill him.

The Hunters were a couple of spear-throws behind him. He dashed into the scrub by the burn where they couldn't see him, and as he did, rain started to fall and soon the ground was slippery beneath his feet.

Hurdling fallen logs, crashing through hazel scrub, he darted through the alders, and took to the water, slipping and stumbling between the pools, leaving no scent for the hounds. He could hear them, closer now—above him, driving him further downhill towards the village—and more people to chase him. He paused mid-stream, saw a rock on the village side, scrambled up the bank, leaving plenty of tracks for the hounds, stepped onto the rock, pivoted and leaped back across the burn.

The trees gave out on that side. Less cover. Gorse and tussocky grass and bog leading down to the shore. He slithered under a clump of gorse, ignoring the sharp thorns, rose to a crouching run and lurched across the slope below, sinking to his ankles in the bog.

As Bhòid reached the shore and sped across the shingle, there was a cry above him. The Hunters had seen him and soon enough the hounds would, too. The tide was running south, away from the chase, hard and rough. Drowning might be an easier death than letting the dogs catch him, but he must save himself for Sulaire's sake.

Breath coming in hoarse gasps, heart bursting in his chest, he pounded on. The dogs were in full cry now, their baying drawing closer, and there was nowhere to hide. His eyes darted from side to side as he ran, looking for something, anything to help him. *Merak*, he cried in his heart, *Feorag!* As if the gods had heard him, he saw, further down the shore, a log caught in an eddy, knocking against a spit of rocks running out from the shore. He put on a frantic burst of speed. Hurtling into the water, he waded towards the log and grasped it with one arm.

Clutching his sickle in one hand, he shoved off, kicking into deeper water until the tide took him. Men and dogs bounded into the sea after him. A spear grazed his leg. Another bruised his buttock before falling into the water. Then the tide, whipped by the north wind, carried him southwards faster than the Hunters and dogs could run along the shore.

He floated out of reach, the sounds of the hunt fading behind him, and as his terror ebbed, the pounding of his heart was replaced with a shattering emptiness. He was alone on the winter-cold water, the rain like hard needles on his back, stippling the dark grey swell. Wind and tide swept him on out of Beaver territory and into the sea loch. His teeth were chattering, his hands were blue, his buttock ached, and the salt water stung his leg. He'd have to come to land soon.

Lifting his head, Bhòid could see smoke on the eastward shore—Hunters from the Falcon Clan most likely, camping out in their hunting runs. Thrall-marked as he was, if they found him, they'd take him back to the Beavers to be killed because he'd killed Athru. He turned to the westward shore—a land of ghosts where dense forest came down, unburned, almost to the water's edge. Gritting his teeth, kicking feebly to keep some warmth in his body, he floated on, fighting against a sudden wave of drowsiness.

When he raised his head again, the rain had eased, and he could see a little further to where the loch split into two narrows around the rising slope of what looked like an island. An island dark with forest, an island where no one went. There was no sign of smoke. No movement on the shore. With one last effort, he slanted the log across the tide, kicking desperately into the lee of a spit that sheltered a little bay.

His feet touched bottom, but, as he lost his balance in the backwash of a wave, his belt snapped. Sulaire's bag and his kilt floated long enough for him to grab them, but his sling was swept out of reach.

He floundered up the shore and stood staring at the bleak emptiness of the place. No charred sticks from a fire. Not the smallest hut for visiting hunters. Nothing but the menace of the forest ahead of him.

The wind was cold on his naked back and the light was fading. He must have food and shelter. He found a few whelks, knocked them open with a stone and swallowed them, grit and all. Then he looked around the shallow bay. A large burn emptied onto the shore, fringed with alder, the forest deep behind it. There was no staying here, where a passing group of Falcon Hunters might see him across the water.

Shaking off his fear of the ghosts in the forest, he headed up the burn until the water ran sweet. There was a faint shaft of light where a sycamore had fallen, its mossed root-mass forming a roof over a small hollow, and he crawled under it.

Inside it was too dark to see. He didn't dare to open Sulaire's bag in case he dropped something and never found it again. Burrowing into the rotting leaves at the base of the hollow, he laid his head on the bag and drew his damp leather kilt over his shoulders. The root-mass above him dripped, and the forest creaked and rustled around him, and he was cold to the bone. A fox barked in the distance and a little creature screamed nearby—a mouse caught by an owl.

Bhòid turned his mind away from the mouse's small death, but he couldn't sleep for the images gibbering in his mind—Athru's dead face as he lay in the burn—the blood on Sulaire's arm—Ead's shrieks, the baying of the hounds—blood seeping from Athru's forehead—Sulaire's cry, the sound wrenched out of her, telling him to go.

Nearby, the burn went on running over the rocks. At last, listening to the familiar sound, he went to sleep.

9

FLAME

BHÒID WOKE, SHIVERING. Maybe it was already dawn, but here under the roots there was no light at all. The darkness of the forest pressed chill and dank against his eyes and his chest until he could hardly breathe for terror. He cowered in his shelter while raindrops splashed onto his face and his hands and the wet leaves beneath him. Hungry and cold, his bruises throbbing, he lay whimpering, waiting for a dawn that never came, waiting for the evil spirits that dwelt in the depth of the forest to stifle him. Words hammered in his mind, *You're nearly a man, act like a man. No Hunter would be so afraid of the dark.* But he wasn't a man yet, and he'd never be a Hunter now. He was just a boy of fourteen summers, shuddering with fear.

His breath faltered as if the air itself was clutching at his throat. *I'm dying*, he thought, but as he did, a drip fell onto his nose, and he sat up, startled. He almost felt Sulaire putting her finger on the tip of his nose, as she did when she wanted to tease him. He could almost hear her crying out, *I'll live.* The memory of her voice steadied him and the dark seemed a little thinner.

He scrabbled among the leaves for his sickle and the bag and crawled out of his shelter. Outside the light was stronger, and he followed the burn downwards. As he came close to the edge of the forest, he realised it wasn't actually raining now; the drips were from last night's rain.

From where Bhòid crouched among the last of the trees, he looked over the boggy ground, across the strait to the shore beyond. The strait was so narrow he could almost have slung a stone to the other side. The *Narrows.* So narrow, and yet so far to the other side. The *Far Shore*, he said to himself, but the name felt wrong—as if he was pushing Sulaire further away. Across the Narrows, a hidden sunrise painted the clouds red. *Red sky in the morning, Hunter's warning,* he thought: storm before nightfall, the *Sunrise Shore* warning him in time to prepare himself.

Why was he standing here naming, when there was so much to be done? Because naming was knowing, the beginning of making paths he could follow without losing his way on this island, if it was an island. *Eilean*. Naming what he could see. Across the *Narrows* lay the *Sunrise Shore*. The side on which he stood, the *Eastern Shore of Eilean*. The little cove where he'd come ashore last night, *Bhòid's Bay*.

Tasting the words on his tongue, he felt less alone, as if the place might be friendly after all. All the same, he couldn't stay on this shore, not where any Hunter passing on the other side might see the smoke if he made a fire. He must leave this dark Eastern Shore, follow Narrows Burn into the heart of Eilean. Maybe on the western side there'd be somewhere he could safely light a fire. But how could he light a fire in this wet place?

It was time to open Sulaire's bag and see what she'd given him. He worked patiently at the wet knots in the string that bound it. She'd oiled the leather carefully and when the knots came free everything inside was dry—a bone awl and needle, a small knife, a medicine horn sealed with wax, a handful of dried berries and hazelnuts and a sprig of rowan to ward off evil. And a small piece of flat birchwood, with holes already drilled. A fire-board. With an elderberry spindle, he could start a fire if he could ever find dry kindling on this dripping island.

His bruised buttock ached. Perhaps Sulaire had put something in the medicine-horn. Scraping the beeswax from the mouth of the horn, he stared—tinder fungus kept dry by the wax. The fungus would help him start a fire, and once started, he could carry the spark in the fungus all day if needed. It must have taken her days to sew and oil the bag so that it was almost waterproof. How had she known what he'd need at the end of what started as an ordinary day? Was she truly blessed by the Goddess?

Bhòid ate one nut, a single berry, just for the comfort of it, but he knew he must keep the rest for times when there was nothing else. Tomorrow he must travel up Narrows Burn, through the dark forest, to see what lay beyond. Without sling or spear he couldn't hunt, so he'd need food to last him several days.

There was no sign of movement across the strait. Crawling low over the boggy shore, he cut rushes with his sickle, slunk back to the edge of the wood and spent the day weaving two misshapen baskets. He'd only just finished when the storm broke—sheets and rivers of lightning, thunder crashing over his head. *Perkwunos*, he prayed, *forgive me if I've angered you.* He flattened himself against the nearest tree as rain lashed against his skin.

As suddenly as it had started, the storm ceased, and a shaft of evening light played over the Sunrise Shore. He crept down to the water and prised mussels from the rocks. When he'd eaten, he filled his baskets with more shellfish and made himself go up the burn to his shelter. He couldn't bring himself to go into its darkness just yet but crouched outside it, clinging to the last vestiges of light.

All morning Bhòid slithered and scrambled up the burn. Unable to gauge the passage of time in the dense forest, he kept stolidly on. Once, he caught the rank smell where a boar had crossed the burn. Later, he saw wolf scat on the bank, but it was days old and he pressed on.

As he climbed, the burn grew narrower and curved away eastwards. He stood there, irresolute—he needed to turn west now, even if it meant leaving Narrows Burn, which reached back like a lifeline to the Narrows. He pressed on, following the rise of the slope until the trees thinned and he came out onto open heath.

South-westwards, the land fell away down a wide, shallow glen, watered by a new burn, and he realised that he'd crossed a saddle between Narrows Burn and *Glen Burn*. On both sides of the *Glen* was open woodland, with a few blackened trunks where fire had raced up the slope in a hot dry summer, but it must have been wildfire, started by lightning—there was no smoke now, or sign of people.

Beyond the Glen, he made out the grey of the sea, an easy walk away. The afternoon sun gleamed on the shore. The *Western Shore of Eilean*. It really did seem to be an island. Across the water, a spit of land, where the sun would soon set, the *Sunset Shore*. Far enough away that if he made a fire the smoke wouldn't be seen.

Heading down the Glen, he came to another burn that tumbled down from the heights and formed a pool before running down the hill to join Glen Burn. Hazels and a big sycamore and a stretch of green grass grew beside the pool. There were stones for building, and a sheltered hollow under a bank guarded by a rowan tree, where he might start some sort of home, a Baile.

Hurriedly he gathered fallen branches and stacked them into a rough shelter against the bank. Cold and hungry, he heard himself whimpering as he doled out a few shellfish and three of the hazelnuts. *Be a man*, he said to himself fiercely. *Stop snivelling.* But still a tear ran down the side of his nose. How could he survive with no fire, no proper shelter, so little to eat, and only damp moss to sleep on? If only he had fire. He heard a chattering above his head. Looking up, in the last light, he saw a squirrel in the rowan.

'Oh, Feorag,' he said crossly, 'if only you were a strong totem. Wolf might give me food. Eagle might show me the way. What can you give me?' As soon as he'd spoken, he felt ashamed, but it was too late. The squirrel turned its back, flourished its tail, a flash of red in the last of the evening light, and disappeared into the darkness as if a fire had been smothered. Kneeling below the tree, Bhòid placed two of his hazelnuts on a flat stone as a gift. 'I'm sorry, Feorag,' he called.

There was no answer, only the darkness deepening and the rain starting to fall again.

In the morning, the hazelnuts were gone from the stone but there was no sign of the squirrel. A light rain was falling, blanking out everything but the small dell Bhòid stood in. He was alone in a grey, wet world. He felt a sob rising in his throat, but he swallowed it. If Feorag was gone, it was his own fault, and he must do something to win him back.

Laying a hazelnut and two berries on the stone—more than he could really spare—Bhòid set about building a proper hut. For two days, mostly in the rain, he worked with sickle and knife, cutting hazel rods and bracken and nettles, gathering sticks and branches. He drove the stronger rods into the damp earth, split the thinner ones into wands, thrashed the nettles against a rock until they were supple enough to lash the rods and wands together for the frame of a small domed hut. He wove the sides with willow, laid sticks across to make a rack, then thatched the roof above with grass and bracken until it was almost watertight.

On the second evening, Bhòid laid twigs and lichen and dry grass over the rack to catch whatever warm air rose from his body. Then he squatted in the door of his hut and looked up into the rowan. For two days he hadn't seen the squirrel. There was little left to eat—a few mussels, a handful of sorrel that felt chill and damp in his stomach, a couple of nuts. He was close to exhaustion, and if he didn't get a fire going soon, if the weather turned again to a late winter, he'd die of cold. He pushed the thought aside. He mustn't die.

Breaking open a handful of mussels, he laid half of them on the stone with Sulaire's sprig of rowan and one of the nuts.

'Feorag,' he prayed, 'your tail is red as fire. Please help me to light a fire.'

In the grey dawn, the rain had eased but water dripped from the trees and through Bhòid's roof. He was blue with cold and afraid. *Feorag hasn't answered my prayer*, he thought. Then he looked at his shrine and saw that the food had gone. The squirrel must be nearby, but hiding, testing him. Hungry as he was, he laid the last nut on the stone.

With nothing in his belly, he made his way downstream to a small pool where the burn curved under the roots of an ash. He lay beside the water all morning, watching, trying to ignore his own shivering. At last, he flicked one small trout out of the water and wolfed it down—skin, bone, innards and all.

He felt a faint warmth on his back and looked up. The rain had stopped, and the sun was shining fitfully. As he hurried back to the hut, the sun came pouring through a gap in the clouds. Taking the kindling from the rack in the hut, he spread it on a flat rock in the sun.

While it dried, Bhòid foraged nearby. He found three large snails and grubbed up a few pignuts and orchids and piled small rocks into a hearth. When, late in the afternoon, the kindling was dry, he chose an elderberry stick for his spindle, set his fire, and started to twirl the spindle in the fireboard. Twirl and twirl and twirl until he could feel blisters starting on his hands. He kept on until a thread of smoke rose from the board and a spark fell into his tinder. He blew until a flame sprouted, then he fed it with wisps of grass, then bigger twigs and sticks.

As the flames licked upwards, he pushed the food he'd gathered into the edge of the fire. When it was charred, he flicked the snails and roots out with a stick, and ate them as soon as he could handle them. The hot food burned his tongue and flooded his chest with warmth.

Just as he was about to cram the last morsel into his mouth, he remembered Feorag and laid the warm end of root on the stone. There was a flicker of movement in the leaves of the sycamore, and Feorag scuttered out onto a branch and looked down at Bhòid, a point of flame reflected in each of its dark eyes. Raising his hands in a gesture of thanks, Bhòid turned to the fire, raking the coals together and covering them with stones before crawling inside his hut.

10

THE LAME WOLF

TWO MORNINGS LATER, Bhòid set out to see what lay on the Western Shore. He took his baskets and two cherry-wood spears that he'd trimmed and then hardened in the fire. Ahead of him the Glen stretched down to the sea, empty of movement. Perhaps there was no clan there. Perhaps he would be safe.

He paused on the lip of the dell, reluctant to leave his fireplace, his hut, Feorag, but the wind on his naked back urged him on. He must have more clothes. If he was ever to make a place where it would be safe to bring Sulaire, he needed to build a house—big enough for two people, a fire and some stores. He needed hides for clothing and bedding, meat to smoke for winter, antlers or bone to make tools. With no sling and only fire-hardened spears, he couldn't hunt any animal bigger than a badger—and they were hard to find.

A big fish, though, might give him enough gut for a snare.

He found a deer-track running close to Glen Burn and jogged down it. As he drew closer, a long, shallow bay stretched before him. Beyond the sand, lay a wide expanse of mud-flat and the air was full of curlews crying. At the northern end of *Wide Sands*, Glen Burn poured through a wood into a small cove. Later he could build a fish trap there.

Near the burn he found a small overhang and stacked firewood there to keep dry. Then he went down to the cove with his spear and waded into the water. There was nothing big enough for what he needed. When he was too cold to bear it any longer, he speared a couple of small fish for supper, left the water and got a fire going under the overhang.

In the morning, while he was gathering periwinkles, he saw a shape wallowing in the waves near the shore. A seal! A seal that he had no way of killing. Then he saw that it was already dead, rolling in the water. Wading out, he grasped it by the ear-holes and pulled it into shallow water.

It had been dead for days and it stank, but apart from a badly torn flipper its hide was sound.

When he slit open its belly with a sharp shell, the stench was so foul he had to turn away and vomit. Seagulls and crows gathered, and he threw them the heart and liver to keep them quiet. Then he pulled out the whole gut and shoved it underwater to work on it—squeezing out the contents, filling the stomach with water and sluicing it through the intestines. When it was clean enough, he looped the whole thing round his body to keep it from the birds while he dealt with the carcass.

All day he worked to skin the seal, scrape the remaining flesh from the hide, wash it in the sea, and then stretch it on the sand as best he could with only rocks to weight it. It was growing dark, but his stomach was churning too much to eat. He was so cold and tired that he used a little of the precious tinder-fungus to light a fire quickly and cowered by it under the overhang.

Next morning, when the sun had warmed the pelt, he smashed open the seal's skull and used its brains to soften the skin, working in the oily mess with his hands. When he'd finished, the pelt was stiffer than he'd hoped. He must kill something big enough, something with plenty of fat or a large brain. That meant making a sling. He cut a square from the thinner skin of the seal's belly and chewed it until it was soft, poked four holes in the corners with his awl and threaded through two lengths of gut.

Choosing several smooth stones from the shore, he cast them quickly to get the feel of the new sling. Confidence flowed through him at the familiar swing and snap of the cord, the thunk of the stones on a tree trunk. But, as the daylight started to fade, suddenly he was afraid. The tinder-fungus wouldn't last forever. He must get back to the Baile tonight, light a fire and keep it going. Struggling into the seal-skin, he packed its gut into one of his baskets, filled the other with shell-fish, and set off up Glen Burn.

The night was clear, a slice of crescent moon showing him where to put his feet. As he headed north-east, the stars of the Great Bear Merak rose above the hills. By the time he reached the Baile, the moon had set and he was travelling by the glimmer of starlight, the sound of water and the rise of the land. When he stumbled into the dell there was no fire glowing on a hearth to welcome him, no sound from the squirrel.

He felt his way into his house, built the tent of kindling and wood by touch, fumbled the last of the fungus out of the horn, blew on it, and thanked the gods when a spark caught his tinder. When he'd cooked some mussels, he banked the fire carefully. In his sealskin, stiff and stinking as it was, he felt warmer than he'd felt yet on Eilean, but tired, and so alone.

He needed more tinder fungus. Soon. More food. Soon. A better house, a boat to bring Sulaire home to Eilean. And what was he bringing her to? There'd be no one to pay her in food for her sewing or healing. No songs or dances or stories round the fire on winter nights. No other women to stave off the loneliness and fear when he was away hunting. No one to help if one of them was sick or injured. Outcasts, who could never go to the Gathering, never find mates. What if one of them got ill? What if one of them died?

His head spun and his belly ached. He crawled outside and was sick. After that, he felt a little better. So far, he'd done well for a boy on his own in a strange place. A small hut to sleep in. A sealskin, spears, a sling. Feorag. For the rest, when he found Sulaire, she'd help him to think. *Leave the rest to the gods*, she'd say. Listening to the memory of her voice, he drifted into sleep.

Bhòid was taking a morning piss when Feorag squealed above him. He smelled the wolf before he saw it, and froze, the hair rising on the back of his neck. Then he saw the grey shape slinking through the bushes, the sun dappling its brindled hide. As it paused to look at him, he saw it was an old she-wolf in pup. Then she moved on, lame in one foot, her belly swinging below her. Not afraid of him, but not likely to attack him, lame and pregnant as she was.

That day, as if the she-wolf had brought him luck, he found a few tinder fungi on birches not far over the Saddle. That night, when he huddled on his rough bracken bed, covered with the stiff seal-skin that left his bare legs cold, he heard a distant howl and wondered if it was his wolf.

Next morning, he rose before dawn, hoping to see her again. The great shape of Merak wheeled above him. As the last stars disappeared, he saw her, skirting the spot where he'd pissed yesterday, as if she respected a boundary. Every morning he pissed on an imaginary line around the dell, marking the territory.

For half a moon, he rose early to make sure he was there if she passed. Nearly every day he saw her returning from her hunting. Always, they exchanged a look. He wondered what had happened to her pack, the young wolves who'd have helped her to care for the cubs when she whelped.

When she didn't come for several days, he thought the cubs must have been born, and then one morning, she was there, slimmer, a dead mole in her mouth. She looked at him for longer than usual and he raised one hand in salute.

A few days later, he followed her. He kept well behind until he almost thought he'd lost her, but then, catching her scent, he wriggled through a tangle of scrub. She lay in a sheltered clearing and a cub crawled out of a hollow under the bank, its eyes just open, and tucked its nose into her side, grunting. Slowly, a smaller cub came out and squirmed up beside its sibling.

The mother raised her head and looked in Bhòid's direction, but made no sound or movement. Surely she knew he wouldn't hurt the cubs.

That evening, he took a trout to the lair. It was empty; the she-wolf was out hunting. He eased out of the bushes until he could place the fish on a rock. When he crept back the next morning it was gone.

If the mother was there when he took food to the lair, she merely turned her head to where he hid, accepting his presence, but never taking his offering until he'd left. All the same, when she passed in the mornings, he could have sworn she smiled at him.

As the cubs grew older, she regurgitated food for them, but he knew that would leave very little for her. Every evening, Bhòid brought them something—the ears and offal of a hare killed with his sling, a couple of mussels broken open. As the cubs ventured farther away from the lair, he saw that the bigger was a dog, the small one a bitch. The dog-cub was rougher, got more food and pushed the little bitch aside.

One day, when the she-wolf was hunting, Bhòid placed some fish guts at the edge of the clearing and waited nearby. After a while the dog-cub came out, snuffing at the smell, saw him, jumped back, stopped, sniffed, looked at the boy again. Bhòid held his breath. The cub crept forward, gobbled the mess of guts, then leaped back out of reach. The little bitch looked on timidly.

For half a moon more, he watched the cubs grow. Then, one grey morning, hunting nearby, he heard a shrill yelping: one of the cubs screaming in terror, and a terrible growling. Grabbing two stones from his pouch, he ran towards the den.

A bear was lumbering away across the clearing. One of the cubs was in its mouth, struggling feebly. Bhòid slung a stone and caught the bear behind the ear, and it turned, snarling, towards him. As Bhòid backed towards the scrub, ready to shin up the nearest tree, the mother galloped out of the brush and leaped across the clearing. The bear reared up, and with a single swipe of his great paw flung her against the crest of a large rock. The boy slung his second stone, hitting the bear's nose. Flinching, it ambled off, the cub hanging limply from its mouth. There was nothing Bhòid could do.

The mother lay twisted and whimpering. When he moved quietly towards her, she looked at him, her eyes full of a dull pain. The fall had broken her back. He sat quietly, meeting her eyes, until something passed between them—trust. She lay there panting, watching him, waiting.

Bhòid nodded and gently moved away. He crawled into the lair, crooning softly, and found the bitch cub, teeth bared, snarling against the back wall. Grasping her by the scruff of her neck, he swung her against his chest, one hand holding her paws so she couldn't scratch, the other clamping her jaws shut.

Holding her tight, he walked back to the mother, who feebly tried to raise her head.

'May you have good hunting with Ullr and Sky Wolf,' Bhòid said. 'I will look after your cub.' As he felt the tears on his cheeks, he started singing, half-choking at first, then stronger, making a hunter's chant to help her on her journey. He sat nearby, holding the wriggling cub until, after a while, the mother jerked and lay still.

Heartsore, he wondered if he should flay the mother for her pelt. Surely her spirit would give it willingly to protect him and her cub, but he recoiled from the task, and before he could make up his mind to it, the grey morning turned to rain. The first thing was to keep the cub safe and warm. He carried her back to the Baile. If only one could live, he was glad it was the little bitch: she was more likely to stay with him.

When he softened some dried fish in his mouth and tried to feed her, she whimpered and nipped, but he held her firm. 'Caraid,' he said, 'be quiet, Caraid. You are my friend now—*Caraid*.' Exhausted, the cub fell asleep in his arms.

Tomorrow, he'd start training Caraid. Tomorrow, he thought, he'd lay out a house to bring Sulaire to. Already it was taking shape in his mind—the foundation of stones, the sturdy rods, the wattle daubed with mud to keep the wind out, a smoke hole, and plenty of thatch. He'd build it in the lee of the gorse bushes and make a thorn-brake, a proper home-place, a true Baile.

11

DISSOLVING THE DARKNESS

HER HEART THUMPING, Sulaire watched Bhòid disappear into the scrub, Hunters and dogs after him. But there was nothing she could do to help him, and she forced herself to stop watching after him, to turn back to where Athru lay still, his head against the rock he'd struck, his feet in the burn. His face was grey and a little blood trickled from his forehead and into the water. Kneeling beside him, she laid the contents of her pouch on the ground—strips of hide, a coil of gut, a knife, a small horn filled with ointment.

Quickly, she bound the gash on her own arm, then held her palm gently over Athru's forehead. There was blood where the skin had broken and a little swelling under her hand. Somewhere, deep inside his skull, she could feel the heat of something worse. Drenching a piece of hide in the stream, she washed the wound and smeared it with ointment to stop the bleeding. She picked up Athru's knife, stained with her own blood, and tucked it between her left hand and his. Placing their clasped hands over his heart, and her right on his forehead, she started to chant, a song to call the evil out of him.

It began to rain. Long before she could call out the trouble inside Athru's head, she could see the Hunters and thralls coming up the hill to where Ead stood waiting for them. Bhòid must have escaped, and the beating of Sulaire's heart eased a little.

Now Ead came puffing up the slope, Hunters and thralls at her heels. How like Ead, Sulaire thought, to have been more intent on seeing Bhòid was punished than whether she could help Athru. As soon as she was close enough, Ead spoke. 'Get away from him,' she said coldly to Sulaire. 'Haven't you done enough harm, you and your brother?'

There was no help for it. Willing a last burst of healing energy into Athru, Sulaire let go of his hand, scrambled to her feet and moved away. From a distance she watched the Hunters rig a stretcher from their spears and tunics. They laid the boy on it, gently enough, and carried him down towards the village, Ead marching ahead of them.

Keeping as close as she dared to Athru, Sulaire limped after them, trying not to slip on the wet ground. She could see Athru's right arm dangling limply from the stretcher, and wished someone would lay it more comfortably on his chest, wished that someone would cover his face to protect him from the rain.

When they neared the village, Ead set up an angry ritual wailing that brought the rest of the Clan running to see the trouble. As the Hunters stopped outside the Headman's house, his mother Cosanta came hurrying out, keening and snatching Athru's hand to her chest so that she rocked the stretcher.

Softly, thought Sulaire, *softly*.

Fiada strode across the meeting-place and gazed down at his son, taking a deep breath and steadying himself. 'Take him out of the rain,' he said to the Hunters, following the stretcher into the house, Cosanta and Ead after him.

When the Hunters came of the house, they huddled with the other bystanders under the eaves, waiting for news. Sulaire sat quietly near Fiada's doorstep, chanting under her breath, calling to Athru, wherever he was walking in the spirit world.

At last Ead and Fiada came out of the house. They didn't notice Sulaire where she sat in the shadows. 'Can you heal him?' Fiada asked Ead quietly, so that the little crowd of bystanders wouldn't hear. 'You might get his mother's hopes up, but tell me the truth.'

Sulaire saw Ead's eyes widen, saw her hesitate, and thought, *She's afraid. Afraid of losing face if she can't heal the Headman's son.* Then the Wise Woman's eyes fell on Sulaire, she drew her head back, and spoke loudly enough for the bystanders to hear. 'This girl and her brother drove his spirit out of your son. Her brother—a thrall—struck him. He fell and hit his head on a rock. The brother ran away like a coward, and your son can't come back to himself while the sister is near. She must be outcast.'

When Fiada looked down at Sulaire, she met his blue eyes, unwavering. He turned back to Ead. 'She's just a girl,' he said.

'A girl who usurps the power of the Goddess. I warned you. The twins have brought us nothing but trouble. She must pay for the harm done to your son.'

Fiada shook his head, 'As Headman, I cannot pass judgement on the girl until I have heard her speak.' He bowed to Ead. 'But you are our Wise Woman, and I thank you from my heart for the care you are giving my son. You must be tired. My thrall will carry the best of our supper to your house that you may sleep soundly and be rested when you come to us tomorrow.'

Ead could hardly refuse the honour Fiada was doing her in front of everyone. With a last sharp glance at Sulaire, the old woman gestured to her thrall and walked towards her own house, leaning heavily on his arm, looking, Sulaire thought, truly tired.

When Ead had gone, Fiada looked down at Sulaire searchingly. 'It didn't happen as Ead said?' he asked quietly.

Sulaire shook her head.

'Did anyone else see?'

Sulaire pointed to two of the thralls who stood waiting nearby.

Fiada took them aside, one by one. She saw the first hesitate, as if afraid, but when Fiada put his hand on the man's shoulder, his face cleared and he seemed to speak more freely. When Fiada had spoken to both of them, he called Sulaire and asked her what had happened.

All the while she was speaking, Fiada kept his eyes fixed on her, measuring her words. When she'd finished, he gestured to the bystanders. 'Show them your arm, Sulaire.' Sulaire unwound the blood-stained hide and held out her fore-arm, the cut, long and deep, still bleeding.

Fiada's eyes darkened when he saw it. He raised his voice. 'My son hurt this girl. I have spoken with these two who saw what happened. I have seen the blood on Athru's knife and the gash on her arm. In return, her brother, Bhòid, injured my son badly. He has already made himself outcast and the gods will deal with him as they see fit.' He looked around the small crowd, and spoke clearly. 'Sulaire has done no wrong, and I give her my protection. Now go to your homes. There is no more to see here.'

As the crowd drifted away, Sulaire bowed to Fiada. '*Atlos*,' she said, using the term of respect, 'thank you, *Atlos*, for your fairness.'

He smiled wryly. 'I find it easier to keep a small band together with fairness and truth than with fear and lies.'

She reached for his hand and spoke urgently, 'I did what I could to call the hurt out of your son, but there's more to be done. Much more.'

He looked at her keenly, and she knew he was thinking of the time she breathed life into Parsa. 'What do you think, Sulaire? Can he come back to himself?' It was against all custom for him to speak so respectfully to a thrall, to go on holding her hand, as if he trusted her.

'If someone who loves him calls to him,' she said, 'I hope he can.'

He stood looking at her, as if waiting for something.

She paused. Who was she to tell the Headman what to do, to speak against Ead who bore the mark of the Moon Goddess on her forehead? Ead might curse both Fiada and Athru if Fiada listened to Sulaire. Sulaire made a helpless gesture with her hands, but then she thought of Athru's need, of his parents' grief if their son did not come back to himself, and she spoke. 'Let his mother be beside him day and night. Let her sing the songs of his childhood, tell him his favourite stories, remind him of everything he ever did well. You also, but his mother most, because she bore him in her body.'

Sulaire saw in Fiada's eyes that he understood; but that he couldn't go against Ead's power of cursing and Cosanta's faith that only the Wise Woman should care for her son.

'I'll do what you say,' he decided, 'as if the idea came from me, not you.' He went on, his voice troubled. 'As for you, keep away from Athru, in case it's true that you bring ill luck. If anything else happens, I may not be able to protect you.' The pressure of his fingers tightened on hers, and then he let her hand go.

For all that Fiada had offered Sulaire his protection, the villagers were in awe of Ead, and although they didn't harm Sulaire, they didn't help her either. Spring was a thin time—the nuts gone, the grasses not yet in head, and Sulaire had no one to climb trees for eggs. She couldn't gather enough wood for a good fire, and the Hunter-women no longer paid her to stitch their tunics. But her very coldness and hunger made her feel closer to Bhòid. Somehow she knew he was safe, for now, but he must be cold and hungry, lonely and afraid, like her.

The worst of it was that every day, as Sulaire crept past the Headman's house on her way to forage, she heard Cosanta speaking and singing to her son. Each day her voice grew sharper and louder with desperation and Sulaire ached to know that Athru lay there while the moon turned from full to new, his spirit wandering somewhere it couldn't hear even his mother calling. If she'd been allowed to go to him herself, she thought, she might have been able to reach him, but it was Ead who entered the house every day, though still Athru lay motionless and silent.

Sulaire felt her danger. If Athru didn't wake to himself, even Fiada might blame her. If Ead cursed her formally, then the Clan might demand her death, or might cast her out to live, or most likely die, alone in the forest.

At night, chanting over a few embers in the cold hut, she drew lines in the dirt, lines that went searching for Athru's spirit. She could feel it, lost, trying to return, and she kept calling to keep it near his body.

On the morning of the new moon, Parsa's mother, the thrall woman Traill, came weeping to Sulaire, saying that her son lay ill in their hut. The woman could hardly meet Sulaire's eyes. She stood shifting from one foot to the other as if she was afraid of Sulaire's bad luck or Ead's curses, or both, but she was also desperate—Ead would do nothing to heal Parsa because Traill had so little to pay. She held out a few hazelnuts.

Sulaire looked at Traill, saw how she was already gaunt—heavily pregnant, with a child to feed, and little enough food for any of them. 'Keep the nuts,' she said, 'I'll come.'

The boy was flushed with fever, moaning. Sulaire felt his forehead, looked at his tongue, his eyes, smelt his breath. She made a poultice for his chest and a tea for his mother to give him. Twice a day she rubbed ointments into his neck and shoulders.

After three days, Traill came to Sulaire with her waddling walk, laughing and shouting her thanks. 'He'll live,' she cried, 'he knew me. He crawled into the sun.'

'Hush,' said Sulaire, quickly, glancing round to see who was listening, but it was too late. As the woman went on gabbling her thanks, Sulaire saw a gaggle of thrall-women watching. Sulaire shivered. They'd gossip, word would come to Ead, and Ead would seek to punish her.

Next morning Athru's mother sent a thrall for Sulaire. Sulaire hesitated—if she was called openly to the Headman's house, nothing could keep Ead from knowing of it—but she could feel Athru's spirit calling her, and so she went.

Apart from his fluttering, uneven breath, Athru lay motionless, his body cold, despite the blazing fire. Sulaire put her hand on his forehead, listened to his heart, lifted his lids and looked into his eyes.

Cosanta, reached, almost timidly, for Sulaire's hand. 'Ead cannot wake him,' she said. 'His father and I have talked to him and sung just as you said, but he doesn't come. Can you wake him?''

'Ead will be angry,' said Sulaire, and felt the tremor in her own voice.

'Let her be angry,' said Fiada's deep voice at the door, 'since she hasn't woken my son.' He looked at Sulaire and again she felt trust flowing between them. It was unheard of for the Headman to flout the Wise Woman, but there he was, his blue eyes pleading.

Sulaire took a deep breath, 'First, I must go into the woods.'

'Can I come with you? Is there anything I can do to help?' he asked.

Sulaire shook her head. 'I must go alone. There are herbs I need. Roots and fungus.'

Before starting her search, she washed herself in the stream and prayed to the Goddess. For a long time she wandered the forest, trying to remember everything Oran had said, trying to know the herbs she found through touch and taste and smell. When she returned, she boiled some of the herbs and bark with Athru's flint knife in the pot. Letting the knife cool, she shaved his hair, showing the gash in his skull, still red and angry. She washed his head, made a poultice for his eyes and the wound on his forehead. Throwing other leaves and lichen onto the fire until a tangy smoke filled the house, she rubbed his hands and feet, massaging his pale, damp skin, moving always towards his heart. Lastly, she stroked his face and neck until his ragged breathing grew steadier.

'Let him sleep, now,' she said to the mother.

As she ducked to go through the narrow doorway, she staggered with weariness and Fiada put out his hand, taking her by the elbow to steady her. She could feel his need tingling through the skin of her forearm, and put her hand over his.

'Something has changed in him,' she said. 'Have hope, *Atlos*. Maybe now he will hear when you talk to him.'

Next morning, Cosanta came early to Sulaire's hut.

'He opened his eyes,' she said, tears running down her cheeks.

When Sulaire reached the Headman's house, Athru opened his eyes again, but she could see that he saw nothing.

For five days, Sulaire tended him. On the fifth, he opened his eyes and looked at her. This time she knew that he recognised her, but his eyes were full of terror.

'I won't hurt you,' she said, putting all the warmth that she could into her voice, 'Athru, I will not hurt you.' Understanding seemed to dawn in his eyes and then fade back to dullness. Sulaire left him to his mother's care, went back to her hut and slept for a day and a night.

When she woke, there was a crock of hazelnuts inside the door, and later Cosanta came with a basket of eggs.

'He knew me,' she said. 'He spoke my name.'

Each morning, Sulaire visited Athru, trying to keep out of Ead's way as she made her way through the village. Each day, Athru grew stronger, drank a little more broth, but still she could feel his fear, the resistance in his body, the way sometimes he shrank from her touch. On the fourth day after he'd found his voice, Sulaire heated a smooth rock, wrapped it in hide, and laid it on his chest. Asking Cosanta to hold his feet, Sulaire gently lifted Athru's head. At first, he resisted, but as she stroked his face and neck and shoulders, he gradually relaxed. Her fingers felt for blocked or twisted energy and found a hard, black knot at the base of his skull where an ancient darkness had settled—something that had been with him from birth or before. She held his head, crooning and willing the warmth in her hands to draw out the evil spirit. After a long time, he shuddered violently and lay quiet.

His mother was frightened, but Sulaire could feel that the darkness had softened. The boy turned his head to rest on Sulaire's knee like a baby, sighed and fell into a soft asleep. She sat until early evening, feeling the blackness dissolve into his blood and leave through his breath and skin.

147

When he shifted in his sleep and rolled over, Sulaire got up stiffly. As she walked back through the village, heavy with fatigue, she rounded a house to find Ead sitting in the last of the sun against its wall. It was too late to stop her shadow from falling across the Wise Woman. As she made the ritual gesture to wash out her offence, Sulaire saw not just rage but also fear in Ead's face and felt sorry for the old woman—sensed the weight on her of expectations and customs that she could never quite fulfil—but she herself was tired, so tired. She limped back to her hut, flung herself on the pile of bracken that served as a bed, and found herself shivering all over, as if she had a fever. *If only Bhòid were here*, she thought. *If only I didn't feel so alone.*

12

PARSA AND ATHRU

A FEW DAYS later, Sulaire found Athru sitting on the bench outside the Headman's door as if he was waiting for her, but he said nothing. Now he could call his mother and father by name, haltingly, but no more than that. When Sulaire sat beside him, he kept his eyes down, as though he was puzzling something out.

She held out her hand with the rough stone she had brought and took his fingers, tracing its shape and texture. 'Stone,' she said, 'sharp, point.'

His hand obeyed hers, and then he looked up at her. 'Sulaire?' he said uncertainly.

She smiled, and kept moving his fingers over the stone. 'Stone, sharp, point.'

'Stone,' he said, 'sharp,' and leaned his head back against the wall as if the effort had tired him.

Fiada came out of the house and watched them, a question in his eye.

'He needs time, *Atlos*,' Sulaire said. She hesitated, unsure if she should tell Fiada what to do. 'Take him with you hunting. Somewhere very close at first. Show him how to set a snare. Tell him the words. Make a path for what he knows somewhere inside to come out again.'

Busy with Athru, Sulaire had given little thought to Parsa. Seeing him running about the village, tumbling with the other children and dogs, she'd thought all was well with him, but one day his mother came to her, leading the boy, and asked, 'What's wrong? I speak, but he doesn't answer.'

'Hold him where he can't see me,' Sulaire said, and Traill turned the child towards her and held him close. Sulaire stood behind him and spoke softly. He didn't move. She sang. Still he didn't move. She clapped, and he startled. She sighed.

'The sickness has taken most of his hearing.'

'Ahhh!' cried Traill, 'what has he done to earn the gods' anger? How will he learn if he can't hear?'

Sulaire looked at the boy. He put his hand in hers, his eyes sparkling with some inner fire.

'He's quick-witted and keen-eyed as a little sparrow,' Sulaire said, 'Parsa, the sparrow. I'll take him with me to gather herbs. He can learn by smell and taste and sight.'

If Parsa had lost most of his hearing, his other senses were sharp. The slightest flutter among the leaves, and he'd shin up a tree, swinging himself through the branches to a bird's nest. He had a sixth sense for which pool a trout was hiding in, and was quick to flick it onto the bank. When Sulaire showed him leaves and roots and berries, he learned fast, grinning when he found them by himself. She never had to search for him—he always knew when she wanted him. If the ground was rough or slippery, he'd give her his shoulder to lean on. And already they were learning a new language of hand signs, glances, touch.

Not long after, Traill died, trying to give birth to a baby who never saw the light. Sulaire would have tried to help, but the birth came on at night, and Sulaire knew nothing of it until she heard the keening next morning. She hurried to Traill's hut and found Parsa crouched beside his mother's body, a few thralls gathered round, ready to take her for burial. Parsa looked up at Sulaire with a tear-stained face, and she put out her hand and led him back to her own hut. That night he wailed and couldn't sleep, but when Sulaire lay down beside him, he burrowed into her arms and slept with his face against her neck.

He never spoke. Words had left him, as if now that he couldn't hear them, they no longer mattered, but the sounds of the forest stayed with him. He'd chitter at a squirrel or whistle at a bird—as if, Sulaire thought, the wordless sounds vibrating in his mouth were his true language.

One day, as he sat beside her peeling hazel-wands, a half-wild village dog came limping to Parsa with a festering thorn. The boy took the wounded paw in his hand, pressed very gently, crooning to the dog. When Sulaire gave him a needle, he dug around the thorn while the dog whimpered but lay still. A burst of pus and blood, and the thorn came loose enough for the boy to pull it out. Then, rumbling to the dog in a language of his own, he trudged purposefully down to the stream, the dog limping beside him, until they reached a place where the current met the tide in a small clear pool. When Parsa plumped down in the water, the dog flopped beside him and let the boy wash its foot in the salt water.

Like most of the mongrels who weren't trained for hunting, the dog had no owner. It followed Sulaire and Parsa everywhere, ate what scraps they could give it, fought with the village dogs for more, and scrounged in the woods for grubs. *Cu*, Sulaire called it, Dog.

Another day, while Sulaire was digging in the sand for lugworms, Parsa saw a jackdaw dragging one wing among a tumble of rocks at the end of the beach. Before Sulaire could reach out an arm to stop him, the child was clambering quietly but steadily, making the jak-jak sound of a jackdaw. The bird hunched motionless and let Parsa pick it up. Holding the bird in the crook of his arm, he came back to Sulaire.

A bird, she thought, *how could I heal a bird?* But a tear was stealing down Parsa's face and the bird lay so quietly in his arm, one grey-ringed eye looking up at her. She took the bird, felt the lightness of its body against her, a place below its shoulder where she sensed the weakness. A splint would be too hard to bind to keep a bird's wing still, she thought. But already Parsa was tugging at her medicine pouch, and she saw what he meant. Kneeling, she emptied the contents. The bird stayed quiet while she held its wings close to its body, wrapped it carefully with two long strips of leather, making a knot at its neck, not too tight, and then eased the whole package inside her pouch until only the bird's head showed.

It might die, she signed, but Parsa shook his head vigorously.

For days, Parsa held the jackdaw bundled close to him, fed it worms and dripped water into its beak. When Sulaire freed it from the pouch and the bindings, it limped around after Parsa, dragging its wing. Each day he gently massaged the wing, until one day, the bird hopped up onto a low branch.

As its wing grew stronger, the bird flew and flopped a little farther, though it never managed the other jackdaws' acrobatic flight. Always it came back at night, often with a worm or caterpillar as a gift, and slept by Parsa's head. Jak, he called it—if the harsh cawing sound he made could be a name. But apart from the cawing, the sounds he made to call Cu, and a special call he made to attract Sulaire's attention, Parsa didn't speak.

Sulaire was sitting sewing on a log outside her hut one evening when Athru appeared and dumbly held out a dressed mountain-hare skin. She gestured to the log, and he sat beside her. It seemed strange at first to sit there with Athru, just as she and Bhòid had sat on warm evenings, using the last of the light, but she thought that Bhòid wouldn't mind. He'd hoped once to be friends with Athru. He'd understand that this new Athru needed kindness.

Athru sat silently watching Parsa playing in the dust, and Sulaire realised that he felt shy with the child nearby. She looked at Parsa. Almost at once, he caught her gaze, and came to her. She put one finger on his cheek and he nodded and melted away, Jak fluttering above him, Cu trotting beside.

'You have no need for words with him?' Athru asked.

His words came slowly, with a kind of roughness, as if they were unfamiliar in his mouth.

'He understands me without.'

'You are kind, Sulaire,' he said, and paused. 'Was I cruel?'

'Not you, Athru,' she said slowly. 'Something in you. Something that's no longer there.'

'Was I cruel to you?'

'Something born in you, I think. Not your fault.'

'Was I cruel to you?' he persisted.

She showed him the scar where he'd gashed her forearm.

He looked stricken.

'Don't blame you-as-you-are-now. It wasn't this you that did it.'

He sat there, tracing a pattern in the dust with his foot. 'You had a brother?' he asked.

'My twin, Bhòid.'

'Where is he now?'

'You really don't remember?'

'No one has told me what happened.'

'You were jealous of Bhòid.' Seeing the trouble in his eyes, she put her hand on his arm. 'Athru, this was the old you. Always trying to outdo Bhòid—to show him he was just a thrall, and one day you would be Headman.' He looked at her intently. 'There were many things,' she went on, 'but I think this was the hardest for you … One day when we were foraging with the children, an old bear came out of the woods.' She paused.

'Tell me.'

'You shouted, "Run!" and you ran. You and two of the bigger thrall-boys.'

'And Bhòid didn't?'

'He held the bear off with his sling while the children and I threw sticks and stones …'

'And?'

'Fiada guessed something of what had happened, and you were shamed.'

'My father knew that I'd run from my totem?'

'Anyone might run from a bear,' Sulaire said. 'I would have run if I could.'

'I remember. There's a lot I don't remember, but I remember that. I'd prayed to Merak. I wanted the most powerful totem. On the Night of the Totems he came. He chose me. I failed him.'

He shivered, as if at a nightmare, stroking the bear-claw he wore on his chest.

Remembering the salmon struggling in the bear's mouth, Sulaire held her tongue. Who was she to question the granting of a totem? How would it help Athru to think that he might really be Salmon, the bear's favourite prey? The thing was done now. She held her tongue.

'What happened after?' he asked.

She couldn't tell him that he'd threatened to take her as his second woman. 'One day, when I didn't answer as you wished, you struck at me with your knife. Bhòid lost his temper and butted

157

you. You fell and hit your head on a rock. Ead set the Hunters to chase him with their dogs but he got away.'

'Safely?'

Her eyes looked far away. 'Yes,' she said, firmly. 'Yes, he's safe.'

'How do you know?'

'It's the twin bond, from before we were born.' She gestured to her left leg. 'When I got the wasting sickness, he saved my life.'

'You miss him.'

'Yes.'

'You should be angry with me.'

'No,' she said. 'Anger sickens the soul. You were angry, Athru. And now that that's gone, you're ...'

'What?' he said.

She wanted to say, 'You have a chance to be someone else,' but it sounded heavy. Instead, she smiled sideways at him. 'You're almost nice.'

He laughed shakily, stood up and rummaged in the pile of firewood next to her hut. When he'd chosen a piece, he sat down beside her again, whittling at the wood with his knife while she went on with her sewing.

At dusk Parsa returned, staggering under a big armful of wood. Athru helped him to stack it neatly, then held out his fist to the child. When Parsa held out his open palm, Athru placed something in it and the child ran to show Sulaire—a small nub of wood, carved roughly, but recognisably, into the shape of a jackdaw.

13

THE CALLING OF THE SALMON

SOMETIMES SULAIRE DOUBTED herself. The pictures she saw in her mind—no, not pictures— more the glancing light when the sun shafted through a dark cloud onto stormy water and then was gone again; the echo of a bird song when the song was over; the touch of wind on the cheek— moments when knowing crumbled as hot coals crumble in a fire, and yet there had been a glow in the coals. She hung on to the memories of that glowing. That she had saved Parsa's life. Brought Athru back to himself. That Bhòid was alive.

As spring turned to summer, the rain fell on many days and the wind blew from the north. In the mornings, when she rose stiffly from the pile of bracken she shared with Parsa, or in the evenings when her leg ached from the day's work, or when she passed Ead and saw the hatred in her eyes—on those days there was only cold ash. She hadn't *seen* early enough to save Bhòid. Parsa was deaf. Ead would stop her from going to the Gathering that year. She wouldn't see Oran, wouldn't learn from her in the healing hall.

And Athru was slow to gain his strength. He moved more slowly, avoided the rough games of the older youths. When Sulaire passed his mother, Cosanta turned her eyes away. Fiada himself seemed more distant, as if he too was disappointed in Sulaire.

She was cooling her feet in the stream one evening, the early summer light shining through the alders, when she heard someone on the trail above her. Before she could get out of the way, she saw Fiada crossing the ford alone, a roe buck slung over his shoulders. He didn't stop, didn't seem to see her.

'*Atlos*,' she called, and he turned. She scrambled to her feet and stood before him, head bowed. 'Are you angry, *Atlos*?'

'Athru,' he said. 'You woke him, but he's so different. He doesn't want to hunt. He finds it hard to kill anything.' He paused. 'A coward can't be Headman.'

'He's not a coward.'

'He starts at every noise.'

'His spirit was lost for a long time. These things are slow to heal.'

'Or was he always a coward? Tell me, what happened that day in spring? Why was he ashamed? Tell me the truth.'

She glanced away, but there was no help for it. 'There was a bear.'

'Yes?'

'*Atlos*,' she pleaded, 'anyone might run from a bear.'

'Not my son. No man runs from his totem.' Fiada's face darkened. 'The gods know I'd rather my son died than be a coward.'

A chill ran down the back of Sulaire's neck and she made the sign to avert evil, but all she said was, 'Take me to the Gathering with you, *Atlos*. Let me ask Oran. She has the Sight. She'll know what to do.'

'Ead will forbid you coming to the Gathering. She'll say you usurped her role as Wise Woman and that's why my son can't hunt.'

He turned away, but she grasped his sleeve, 'Please, *Atlos*. She couldn't heal him. I did. You know that I tell the truth. But I am young, I know so little. Only Oran can tell me what more needs to be done.'

He bit his lip. 'Then ask Oran how I am to protect the Clan from Ead's curses,' he said. His face was pale.

There was a real skill to Fiada's leadership, Sulaire thought, watching him lift Ead into the place of honour in the centre of the first canoe, in front his own woman, Cosanta. As the thralls pushed the boat further out, he leaped into the stern, taking one of the paddles himself, so that Ead was already far out on the water when Athru helped Sulaire into the second boat. He tossed Parsa up to sit between her knees, Jak clinging to his shoulder. Cu whimpered and bounded in the water, trying to leap aboard. Athru touched his head, and whistled to the dog, before running up the sand to join the shore party that would travel overland.

The boats skimmed swiftly southwards with the run of the tide, the paddlers—the strongest young Hunters—singing to keep the beat, the north wind helping them on, a light scud of rain on their backs.

At mid-morning they came in sight of what looked like an island across a narrow stretch of water to the west. There was no sign of people, no huts, no smoke, but Sulaire could feel a pull. As the boats drew closer, the pull grew stronger. Bhòid was there. Alive. Watching, she was sure, from the cover of the trees.

She thought of tumbling into the water and trying to swim across, but the tide was pulling them strongly forward and there was Parsa to think of. She mustn't call, mustn't let anyone suspect that he was there. Below her breath she started quietly singing the wordless song she used to sing when they were children. As she sang, the boat passed near a flock of diving gannets, and a single bird flew over her head and drifted away to the west, over the island, and she was sure—almost sure—that Bhòid would receive the message.

With Parsa's hand in one of his and Sulaire's bundle over his shoulder, Athru led them to a spot on the edge of the summer camp near the healing hall where he'd already laid bracken ready for bedding. While Parsa and Cu went looking for firewood, Athru helped Sulaire tie the hides that wrapped her belongings between two trees to shed the worst of any rain. He was intent on scraping a trench to take the water away from the shelter when a sudden splurge of voices cut through the noise of the camp.

'Hey, Athru! Athru!'

'Leave that thrall's work!'

'Scrimmage on the arena!'

'Now!'

He turned and stared at the gaggle of youths lounging towards him, arms round each other's necks. Seeing the look of blank terror on his face, Sulaire realised he didn't remember them, didn't recognise the Hounds of the Bear tribe that he'd trained with these last two summers. She pushed him gently in the chest.

'Pretend!' she said urgently. 'You'll work out who they are when you join the scrimmage. Go!'

He let himself be swept away by the small group of seven or eight of the Hounds, stripped to their kilts, girls and boys. Cuffing and jostling, they half-dragged Athru to the arena near the edge of the Bradan. From a distance, Sulaire watched the rough game of wrestling, throwing some sort of ball, running. She couldn't work out the rules or the aim, if there were any, and Athru was wavering in the midst. Twice he was knocked over, but then he seemed to get the hang of it. He had the misshapen ball in his grasp and was running, and some of the Hounds were cheering him on, until a bigger boy slammed into him and sent him flying. He scrambled to his feet, shaking his head and chasing after the flow of the game.

Stowing her few belongings neatly under the shelter, Sulaire took the moccasins she'd stitched for Oran and walked across to the healing hall.

As before, Oran was standing on the doorstep, waiting. She stroked the fine stitching on the marten-fur moccasins. 'My feet will be warm this winter,' she said gruffly. 'Much has happened,' she went on, looking Sulaire up and down.

'Yes.'

The old woman nodded. 'I heard about the child you breathed life into, and about the price you paid—according to Ead. As for me,' she went on fiercely, looking down at Sulaire's wasted leg, 'whatever Ead thinks, I don't believe that the gods punish us like that. Not for trying to help someone. It just happened that you got the fever.'

She took Sulaire's left hand. The dry, light touch of her fingers traced the lines of the palm. Then the right hand. 'I heard about the Headman's son that you brought back to himself.'

Sulaire dropped her gaze. 'It wasn't me,' she said. 'It was something that came through me. From outside.'

Oran smiled. 'Not many can make the space for it to come.'

'Teacher,' Sulaire asked, 'how do you know all this?'

'I hear things. Traders. People who travel to me with sicknesses that the likes of Ead can't heal. There's little that goes on in the Tribe that I don't hear of. And some things *I see*. As we have said.'

For a while, Oran watched the Hounds, down on the arena, still playing the rough games that would make them strong and agile when it was time for the Boar Hunt at the end of summer. 'He's not the same, that one,' she said.

'Athru?' Suddenly Sulaire was speaking in a rush. 'His mother is angry with me because he's not the same. He hates hunting and killing, and Fiada's afraid that he's become a coward. Ead hates me because I brought him back when she couldn't. And as for Athru—look how he's standing. He's afraid he *is* a coward. I promised Fiada I'd ask you what to do.'

'No,' said Oran thoughtfully, 'he's not a coward. But he no longer wants to hurt things. He was a cruel boy and you brought out kindness in him. You have great power, Sulaire. That's something even I have never done.'

'Then how can I help him not to be afraid?'

The old woman looked troubled. 'Let it be as it is.'

'Teacher,' begged Sulaire. 'I didn't heal him for him to be frightened and unhappy.'

Oran pointed to where Athru was coming back to the meeting-place in the middle of a raucous pack of Hounds eager for the evening meal. 'He'll do well enough' she said. 'Go and eat now, Sulaire. Rest after your journey.' She stroked Sulaire's face. 'And be careful of Ead. Keep out of her way.'

At dawn on Midsummer's Day, Sulaire waited on the slope above the Bradan with the rest of the Tribe as the coming sun limned the eastern hills. On the level space beneath them, a circle of birch poles showed white in the half light. In the centre, a young deer lay bound on an unlit fire on the stone altar. Sagart the High Priestess, her robe daubed with white ochre, stood by the altar, a half-moon of Healers and Wise Women—Ead and Oran among them—standing behind her with lit torches. As the sun rose, casting the shadow of the longest pole onto the altar, Sagart's knife flashed down, the acolytes thrust their torches into the kindling, and the deer's blood flowed into the leaping flames.

When the fire had burned down, the deer's carcase was thrown into the river for the sacred Calling of the Salmon. Throughout the day of fasting, Sulaire worked with the other women preparing for the night's feast. The last of the hazelnuts were ground with berries and deer fat to bake the flat cakes that were always part of this feast. Summer herbs and roots were stewed in clay pots beside the fire and drinking-horns and wooden bowls and spoons scoured clean.

From time to time, Sulaire glanced across to where the Headmen were gathered in the pool below the first rapids, spearing the salmon as they leaped out of the water. On this first day only the Headmen fished, catching enough for the feast tonight, while the other Hunters waited on the shore to prepare the fish. On the arena, the Hounds were practising the steps of the Salmon Dance.

As the feasting began, the aroma of roasting salmon filling the air, Sulaire sat at the edge of the meeting-place. The Hounds served the Great Ones of the Tribe—the boys carrying platters of salmon and filling the drinking-horns with ale and mead, the girls passing bowls of stew and hazelnut cakes. Mathan, Sagart and Oran did not touch the salmon—taboo to members of the Salmon Clan. Instead the boys brought them collops of roasted deer.

When the Great Ones had been served, the Hounds fell to eating what was left of the feast. A chill ran down Sulaire's spine. If she was right about Athru's totem, then salmon was taboo to him, too. She hadn't warned him, and there he was laughing and jostling with the others for the last of the salmon.

As the midsummer light paled in the sky, the young Hounds began their dance, the boys darting round the outer ring, throwing blunted spears from boy to boy so that they flew between the girls who leaped in the inside circle as if they were the salmon flinging themselves up the rapids. Sulaire saw that Athru looked pale, keeping up the steps with grim determination as the dancing whirled faster and faster until all the boys and girls dropped exhausted to the ground.

Instead of falling with the others, Athru staggered away into the dusk, down towards the river. Stealing away from the fire and following him, Sulaire found him down by the water, retching and heaving up all that was in him.

She knelt beside him until he'd finished, then helped him to his feet. 'Athru?' she said.

He stared at her, the whites of his eyes showing clearly in the half-light of midsummer. 'I started to feel sick as soon as I ate the salmon. It must have been left too long in the sun.'

She stretched out a hand towards him. 'I don't think so.'

'Then what? What is it, Sulaire?'

The words almost stuck in her throat, but she forced them out. 'Athru, when the bear came, the Night of the Totems …'

'Yes?'

'There was a salmon, still alive, in its mouth.'

'What are you saying?'

'Maybe … just maybe … who am I to say … could it be that your totem is Salmon?'

He flinched as if she'd struck him, then raised

his fist as if he might strike her. 'My totem is Bear,' he said savagely, almost pushing her aside as he stalked back towards the fire.

14

RUAD

CARAID IN HIS arms, Bhòid looked across the Narrows. There was no one on the water, no sign of fires or people on the Sunrise Shore. To judge by the moon, it would be a few days yet before the Beavers passed on their way to the Gathering. He must wait to know if Sulaire was with them.

'When I bring her,' he thought, and then spoke aloud, as if the sound of his own voice would make it real, 'we may need shelter here.' He would build a small hut, one that could be used later on hunting trips. The fallen tree where he'd huddled—three moons ago, now—was too close to the Burn, too damp, too likely to flood. He found a small clearing near the edge of the forest so he could watch the Narrows as he worked. For five days he waited, building the hut, training Caraid to stay on command, eating raw shellfish rather than risk giving himself away with a fire.

On the sixth day, he saw the first boat passing the small islands a little way north from the Narrows. Two big canoes, two kayaks. Was Sulaire with them? Would he know if she was left behind?

The boats came closer, driven by the tide and a north wind. With rain stinging his face, he could barely see. The boats were bunching up a little to pass through the Narrows, and then they'd be gone. It was too far to see if Sulaire was there or not, if she was alive as she'd promised. He felt sick with his need to know. As the boats drew near a flock of diving gannets, a single bird drifted away from the flock, flew over the second boat, across the water and over his head, croaking.

She was alive. Somehow, she was even going to the Gathering. He clutched Caraid tight in his arms to keep himself from racing down the shore, and stood watching as the boats swept on, out of sight. He'd never felt lonelier.

But there was work to do. A plan to think out. He looked across the water, gauging the distance and the strength of the current. Not swimmable for a girl with a crippled leg. He'd need a boat. When the Beavers came back from the Gathering, the nights would be longer, so there'd be more darkness to cover their escape. Three moons to wait. The leaves were still fresh green, and he must wait until they turned yellow. Before they started to fall, he must be here, ready, with a boat. Putting Caraid down to walk a little, Bhòid set off up Narrows Burn for the Baile.

That evening, while a partridge he'd killed on the way was cooking, he laid out his meagre store of tools. A sling. An antler-horn knife. An awl. A few needles. Gut. His stiff sealskin and a few small pelts. A sickle. He had no axe, no saw, no easy way to make a boat and paddles. Perhaps he could make a small raft like the Beavers used sometimes at low tide in the estuary. No, he thought, a raft wouldn't be safe in the fast tides of the Narrows with only one boy to manage it.

The smell of scorching meat brought him back to himself. He had nearly three moons to work something out. Tomorrow he'd scour the woodland near Wide Sands for anything that would serve. Now he'd eat and sleep. He chewed some of the partridge meat until it was soft and gave it to Caraid. That left little enough for him. His stomach half empty, he lay down by the fire with the cub against his belly and slept.

After days of searching, Bhòid had found nothing he could easily shape into a paddle; no fallen branches the right size and length for a raft, even if a raft was safe. Maybe if he had enough gut and rope, there was a way of binding rushes into a rough kayak—something he could manage more easily on the tide. Next day he daubed himself with mud to keep off the worst of the midges and mosquitoes, and worked knee-deep in the marshes, sawing through rushes with his sickle.

By late afternoon, when his back was aching, he was covered with insect bites and had cut what seemed like a woefully small stack of rushes, he ran down to Wide Sands. High clouds were rising towards the west, but there'd be plenty of time for a swim before the storm broke. Leaving Caraid on the shore, he plunged in. She whimpered a little at first, but quietened when he spoke to her. She was beginning to learn to be quiet when he needed to leave her, to guard his belt and knife and kilt.

He could swim like an otter now, but today, with the storm building and the wind rising, he didn't stay long. As he waded out of the sea, the rain started, great drops pocking the surface of the water. Rain before wind—a bad sign. Turning westwards, he saw the shadow of the coming wind racing across the water towards him. There was something darker in the midst of the shadow—a boat. Grabbing Caraid and his spear, Bhòid ducked behind a rock, watching the boat come closer, yawing as the west wind grew stronger across the southerly pull of the tide.

There was one tall figure in the canoe, sometimes almost swamped by the waves, the tide driving him towards the rocks at the north end of the bay. The canoe was beginning to founder as the man paddled furiously.

A big wave hurled the boat against a rock and it capsized, throwing the man into the water, the boat dragging and tearing against the rocks.

Bhòid dashed from behind the rocks and ran into the water, his knife in his fist, ready to kill the paddler if he had to, as long as he could save the boat. Water sloshed into his face as he breasted the waves. As he neared the boat, the paddle swept past him on the tide before he could grasp it.

It wasn't a man clinging to the gunwale, but a tall, naked boy, an axe raised in his fist.

Neither of them could save the boat alone. 'Together!' Bhòid shouted. 'We can do it together!'

He clenched his knife between his teeth and grasped one end of the boat with both hands.

As the boy tried to get a hold on the other end, a bigger wave knocked him against the rocks and when he staggered upright, his hand was empty. No time to look for the axe. Together, half swimming, half floundering on the rocky seabed, the boys hauled the boat into the shallows and dragged it to the edge of the water where Caraid fidgeted on the sand.

With a last surge of effort, the boys pulled the boat above the tideline. Bhòid turned to the boy, but, as if the time of working together had never been, the stranger snatched up two rocks and stood over the boat, glaring. Slowly, Bhòid stepped back. He must have the boat, but surely, with just the two of them on this island, they should work together. He turned his knife in his hand, hilt towards the stranger to show he meant no harm, but the boy merely raised one arm to throw a rock. Taking another step back, Bhòid held out his other hand, palm open. The stranger stood there, wild-eyed, rocks raised in each hand. Shivering and grey with fatigue, he didn't seem much of a threat. As Bhòid stood there uncertainly, the boy swayed and crumpled onto the sand.

When Bhòid approached cautiously, Caraid close at his heel, he saw an angry gash on the boy's calf, the infection spreading up over his knee. An oyster cut, perhaps. His nose looked as if it had recently been broken—a greenish-yellow bruise spreading over his face. Blood trickled down his chest and arms, where he'd cut himself on the rocks, and he was muttering through pale lips.

Bhòid stood staring down at the stranger, grasping his knife. If it came to a fight when the boy woke up, Bhòid might lose. He couldn't afford to lose the boat. If he killed the boy now with a swift knife thrust to the throat, he could be sure of the boat. But he knew that wasn't what Sulaire would do. Then he saw, beneath the boy's ragged, reddish hair, the tell-tale brand under his ear. Like him, the boy was an escaped thrall.

As he knelt beside the boy, blood from a cut on Bhòid's own wrist—he must have gashed himself on a rock—dripped onto the blood seeping from a cut on the boy's chest. A sign. Since it was meant, it must be done properly. He laid the two wounds together, mingling the blood. Now they were brothers—a bond the boy would have to honour when he woke. As if she too had accepted the boy, Caraid flopped down beside him.

Motioning her to stay, Bhòid ran up the beach to his camp, fetched his sealskin and his pouch of herbs, and ran back. When he rolled the boy onto the seal-skin, he gasped. His back was ripped and bruised. He'd been badly beaten and some of the wounds were infected. No wonder he was sick. No wonder he was hostile and desperate.

As gently as he could, Bhòid pulled the boy over the sand and into the lee of the rocks. Then he dragged up the boat and tipped it over him as a shelter, propping up one side with a stick. It had a great rent in the hide, but it would break the wind and give some cover if it rained. A spear with a beautiful obsidian blade was lashed to the thwarts, a bundle tied to it. Bhòid emptied the bundle to dry the contents—a deerskin cloak and tunic, moccasins, a bag with dried meat, needles and gut.

He set a small fire in the lee of the boat. Water was harder—it took many trips from the stream with a large cockleshell before he was able to trickle enough water into the boy's half-closed mouth. He soaked some hide in the stream and cleaned his wounds, making a poultice of yarrow and comfrey and covering him with the deerskin.

That night, he and Caraid lay against the boy's back to keep him warm, but in the morning he was worse, tossing and raving, his wounds swollen and angry, his whole body burning with fever. Cleaning his small knife in the fire as he'd seen Sulaire do, Bhòid pierced the worst wounds until the pus burst out. He was about to clean them when Caraid started to lick them, growling when Bhòid tried to stop her.

All day he kept the fire going, dribbled water into the boy and laid wet hide on his chest to cool the fever. And all day Caraid lay beside him, licking the wounds.

That night they slept under the boat, and in the morning, the boy was cooler, the wounds less angry, but he was still muttering and thrashing. Again Bhòid and Caraid tended him all day, and on the next morning he woke. At first, he looked wildly about him, but he was too weak to sit, and he fell back, looking at Bhòid in terror.

Bhòid held out his hands, palm up, keeping his distance as Caraid wormed her way forward and licked the boy's hand. His eyes cleared—a bright, wondering blue. 'You helped me,' he said.

Bhòid nodded.

'You could have killed me,' the boy said quietly. Tears started from his eyes and he turned his head away as if ashamed.

'Two is better than one,' Bhòid said gently. 'My name is Bhòid. This is Caraid.'

'They call me Ruad,' the boy said, pointing to his red hair. 'Thank you,' he mumbled, and fell asleep again, one arm flung over Caraid.

Next morning, Ruad was stronger and the boys turned the boat over to assess the damage. The hide was gashed in several places, some of the stitching torn, the lashings loose, a couple of thwarts and wands broken. It would take days, perhaps a moon, to make it watertight, but it was a boat. Bhòid could see how it could be remade. The spear was still lashed to the thwarts.

Suddenly Ruad's face was full of the old anger. 'I had an axe,' he said. 'And a good knife. What have you done with them?'

'Hold on,' said Bhòid, 'hold on!' He fetched Ruad's bag and laid out its contents. Needles, gut, dried meat. 'This is all I found. You dropped the axe in the sea when you fell.'

'The knife was in my kilt-belt,' Ruad said, sullenly.

'What belt? What kilt? You were naked. It must have been torn off by the rocks and waves.'

'It was a flint knife.'

Bhòid groaned. 'And I have no flint. I've found none on the island.'

The boys looked at each other, the promise of easy fire snatched away by the sea.

'Never mind,' Bhòid said. 'I have a fire-board, a little tinder fungus, and you bring a good spear. We're better off than I was alone. But the axe! The axe *would* help. Let's look now, while the tide's out—near the rocks where the boat turned over.'

Again and again they dived, searching with feet and hands among the rocks and sand until, with a triumphant shout, Ruad surfaced with the axe in his fist.

By then Ruad's face was blue, teeth chattering with cold. Bhòid sent him ashore to wake the fire, while he kept diving for the knife as long as he could bear it, but the knife had gone, torn away by Mor, the sea god.

All the same, that night the boys made an offering of fish to thank Mor for saving the boat, for bringing Ruad safe to land, and for giving back the axe.

15

THE WOODEN BOAT

RUAD'S BACK WAS healing, the scabs loosening over the scars. The swelling on his nose went down, but it would always be crooked. Those were the hurts Bhòid could see. There must be other, deeper hurts that went with their making.

Though the boys spoke more or less the same language, many of Ruad's words were different, spoken with a burr. For the first days they said little—words mainly to do with food or tools, fixing the thwarts and lashings of the boat, felling a birch tree and rough-carving new paddles. They worked well enough together and took time to fish and swim in the long, warm evenings.

But sometimes Ruad turned silent and sullen, sitting on a boulder, one arm round Caraid, looking northwards. He never spoke of where he came from. If Bhòid asked a question, his face closed. In response, Bhòid held his own story shut in his heart.

One afternoon, when Bhòid handed one of the paddles to Ruad and took up a stone to start sanding the other, Ruad flung down the paddle. 'The boat,' he shouted, 'always the boat. As if there was nothing else! As if we were going anywhere!' He blundered away across the rocks, shoulders hunched as if there was a storm driving him. Caraid trotted after him a little way, before coming back to Bhòid, whimpering.

'Leave him awhile,' Bhòid said to the wolf-cub, and returned to his sanding.

Every now and then he raised his head to look at where Ruad sat crouched on his boulder. At last, as if the pain in Ruad's very blood was calling to the blood-brother in him, Bhòid scooped up Caraid and made his way across the rocks, gingerly, so as not to poke Ruad's sore places too suddenly. Squirming herself out of Bhòid's arms, Caraid scrambled up beside Ruad and licked his toes.

Ruad fondled the cub's ears absently. After a while, he growled, 'Stop telling me what to do. I'm not your thrall!'

The words bust out of Bhòid, hotter and angrier than he meant, 'Whose thrall are you, then!'

Ruad flinched as if he'd been struck, and turned towards Bhòid, his face twisted with fury. 'My father's,' he cried. 'My own father's!'

'I'm sorry,' Bhòid said, and sat quietly on a rock. Slowly, using gestures where he had no words, Ruad began to speak in shattered phrases, as if he was breaking up the memories like ice on a pool to get to the water beneath.

'As a small boy, I was hungry. Scavenging for food with the dogs. Different from the other boys. Taller. No mother. No father. Red hair. They pelted me with stones. An old woman, Awija, let me sleep in her hut and told me who I was. A trader selling axe-heads had wintered in our village. Tall and red-haired like the woman with him. Ingen, her name was. In spring, the man went on alone and never came back. After I was born, my mother was never strong. She died before I knew her.'

'Mmm,' Bhòid said softly.

Ruad swallowed. 'As soon as I could carry a pack, I left Awija—alone, with no one to help her through the next winter. I ran away with a trader, looking for my father. I wanted so much to have a father, to belong somewhere. To know something of my mother. Sometimes, at night, when I was drifting off to sleep, I thought I could remember her voice, but in the morning, the memory had faded. I wanted to know where my red hair and height came from. After many traders and many beatings, I found my father. Red hair, a voice that sounded as if I'd known it before. His name was Gaoth, he said, meaning *the wind*. Because no one knew when he was coming or going. He had a strange smile. I should have known from his smile.'

'He knew you were his son?'

Ruad shrugged. 'We look alike, but to him I was just a big strong lad who could carry the packs along with his thrall. Once, he was sick. I tended him. When the fever broke, he smiled at me—a real smile. "Ingen's son," he said. He told me they came from far to the east, from the Land-across-the-Water. They ran away together because she was very beautiful and promised to the Headman's son.'

Bhòid sat quiet, waiting.

'Next day he was better, and I was just a thrall again. When we reached the Boar Clan, a village of granite axe-makers, there was another son and a dark woman with a bitter look on her face, as if she'd chewed bogbean. I think Gaoth was afraid of her. Perhaps even afraid of the son, Dubh—a real bully. Gaoth told them I was his new thrall. Of course they wondered—my red hair, my height. That evening Dubh said loudly, in front of the Clan, "If he's your thrall you should brand him." Everyone round the fire laughed at that, something happening on a dull evening. They held me down. Perhaps Gaoth didn't really want to, but in the end, he's a coward. He pulled a stick from the fire and branded me.'

For a while, the boys sat watching Caraid snuffling for crabs under the rocks. The sun was dipping low, the tide was out, and sandpipers were thrusting their beaks into the sandy mud, their reflections stretching behind them across the wet-rippled shore. Bhòid gestured to Ruad. 'Wide Sands,' he said. 'That's my name for it.' He grasped Ruad's hand. 'There'll be no thralls on Eilean if I have anything to say about it.'

'Eilean!' Ruad broke out, half angrily, half in despair. 'What's Eilean? Two boys and a wolf cub sleeping under an overhang and winter coming soon enough. One band of foraging Hunters on your precious Eilean, and we'll be thralls again.'

He wrenched his hand out of Bhòid's, leaped from rock to rock and onto the sand, floundering across the muddy flats, out into the water. He swam so far that Bhòid was afraid that he might not come back. *There must be other things*, he thought, trying to stifle his own anger at Ruad, *worse even than the branding. That broken nose, the beating. They were new when he came.*

Whistling to Caraid, Bhòid went back to their camp and woke the fire. At nightfall, Ruad came back, squatting by the fire without a word. When Bhòid pushed a share of the evening's fish towards him, Ruad wolfed it down as if there was an emptiness in him that could never be filled, rolled himself in his hide and lay down by the fire, his back towards Bhòid.

That night Bhòid woke to find Ruad clutching his wrist, saying clearly, 'Come with me, Cailin,' before slumping back onto the bracken.

Next day, Ruad's face was closed again. He ate more than his share of their morning meal and snarled at Caraid when she licked his hand. All morning he was careless and clumsy and the boys made little progress on the boat. 'There's more to Eilean than this,' Bhòid said firmly. 'Time to go home.'

Sullenly, Ruad helped him to hide the paddles and boat in the undergrowth. As Bhòid led the way up the Glen, Caraid tried to keep up a steady hunter's trot at his heel, but soon she tired and sat down, panting. He slung her over one shoulder for a while, put her down to walk again, slowed his pace to hers, intent on training her. Ruad trudged silently behind.

In the late afternoon, with the sun shining over the green dell of the Baile, Bhòid paused on the lip of the bank above it. 'Welcome to my Baile,' he said to Ruad.

Ruad shrugged, his gaze passing over the tiny settlement, and suddenly Bhòid felt that it didn't seem so much to show—a half-made thorn-brake, a small store-hut, the wattled house where even Bhòid couldn't stand upright. Not much to withstand the winter gales and snow, or to keep out wolves.

'It's my home, Ruad,' Bhòid burst out, 'the place I'll bring …' He broke off. He couldn't speak of Sulaire. Not now, with Ruad stuck in his hard shell of anger—or grief. 'It's not so bad,' Bhòid muttered, 'for one boy alone with no tools beyond a sickle and a small knife.'

A streak of red flashed in the sycamore above and the squirrel scampered along the lowest branch. It stopped just above Bhòid's head, chattering reproachfully. 'I wasn't quite alone,' Bhòid admitted, pointing up towards the squirrel, 'I had my totem. Feorag.'

Ruad snorted. 'A fitting totem for an outcast thrall boy.'

Anger surged up in Bhòid's throat like water boiling over a pot. 'You've been bullied so much, Ruad,' he said fiercely, 'that you've become a bully yourself, with no manners and no feelings and no sense of the gods. There's rain coming. Get the fire lit. There's a hearth in the house.' He flung the last words over his shoulder, and stalked off towards the store-hut.

When Bhòid looked back, Ruad was standing where he'd been left. He looked so white, so lonely, that Bhòid almost went to him, but he was too angry. He busied himself stowing away the smoked fish they'd brought, checking the roof for leaks, taking longer about it than was needful. Choosing three small fillets of fish, he went back to the house where Ruad had the fire going with roots roasting at its edges.

'A bit stingy isn't it,' Ruad said, eyeing the fish, 'when we brought back so much?'

Bhòid stared at him. 'It's summer, Ruad.' He spoke patiently, as if explaining to a child. 'It's warm. Now we can manage with little enough in our bellies, but in winter …' *With Sulaire to feed as well*, he thought, but still he couldn't speak of her. 'We *must* lay in food for the winter,' he finished.

He held some of his fish out to Ruad. 'You're taller than me, and you've been ill. Here. Have it.'

As if ashamed, Ruad pushed Bhòid's hand away, hunched into himself and lay down to sleep.

When Bhòid woke, it was daylight, Caraid was whimpering and Ruad was gone. Bhòid found him a little way up the burn, stuffing a piece of fish into his mouth—fish stolen from the store-hut—looking as though he could hardly choke it down. As he saw Bhòid, Ruad flung down the fish, thrusting his jaw out and clenching his fists, waiting for the blow.

Bhòid turned and walked away.

'Are you afraid to fight me?' Ruad yelled. 'Are you a coward?'

Bhòid looked back at him. 'It's just common sense,' he said levelly. 'You're taller and stronger.

I'm not going to let you beat *me* because *you've* stolen a fish. Whatever's the matter with you, Ruad, you'll have to fight it out with yourself, not with me.'

Ruad's face crumpled. He looked as forlorn as a child, and Bhòid's anger suddenly washed out of him. He went back and put his arm round Ruad's shaking shoulders.

Slowly, as if the words were being wrenched out of him, Ruad started to speak, 'I've never had a home. I don't have a totem. Thralls don't have totems.'

'My sister helped me to find my totem. Feorag is the spirit of fire.'

'You didn't tell me you had a sister?'

Bhòid shrugged. 'We didn't have the words before. It was all about boat and wood and food. And you were so angry.'

'I had a sister, too,' Ruad gulped. 'And a small brother. For a little while.'

'Cailin?' asked Bhòid. It was chilly in the morning air and he was hungry, but things would be better between them when all was told. 'You called out to her in your sleep.'

Ruad nodded. 'When Gaoth left Ingen behind, it didn't take him long to find another woman.'

He spat into the water. 'Dubh, their son, is a year or so younger than me. Cailin, a year younger again. Not at all like Dubh. Kind. She salved my burn after the branding. She looked after Teksla, her little brother—*my* little brother, two summers old. Big, blue solemn eyes. Sometimes when I worked with the boatbuilders she'd bring Teksla down for me to keep him well out of Dubh's way. She knew he'd be safe with me. I whittled him a wooden boat and two little men with tiny paddles. He'd sit in the sand playing beside me until Cailin came to fetch him to sleep. Until …' His voice trailed off.

'Until …?' Bhòid said quietly.

'Until Gaoth promised her to an old man of the Ravens in exchange for the man's daughter. He sold his own daughter to buy a mate for Dubh when he's made man this autumn.' He stared at Bhòid. 'What could I do? I asked her to come away with me, but she said it wouldn't change anything. I'd be a thrall again, and she'd be given to some old man who was over-fond of mead. It's the way of it.'

'Should we go back for her?' Bhòid asked, wondering desperately if there was time to finish the boat, go wherever Ruad needed and be back in time to meet Sulaire as she returned from the Gathering.

Ruad shook his head. 'She'll be gone by now. Somewhere far to the north. The man of the Ravens came for her at Midsummer. The night before Midsummer, Dubh and his friends got into the mead, drunk as badgers, and came down to the water where I was working. I was making Teksla a song about the men in his boat and he was laughing. Dubh grabbed him, ran into the water and started ducking him. I hit Dubh so hard he fell into the water and let go of Teksla. I snatched Teksla up and ran, and Cailin raced down and took him. Dubh's gang dragged me into the water. Dubh held me under. I was sliced by oyster shells. I twisted away, dived under, reached the shore with them running after me. I knocked the first two flying. Dubh's no coward, even if he's a bully. He kept running towards me, but I was too fast, too angry. I dragged him into the water and held him down. Half the village had come to watch the fight. Gaoth's bitter-faced woman was shrieking. Gaoth pulled me off Dubh, thrashed me, kicked me, broke my nose.

'That night, when all the men were drunk, I dragged myself to Gaoth's shed, took a knife, the axe, his best spear, and went down to the shore to steal a boat. Somehow Cailin knew. She was waiting with Teksla on the shore. I asked her to come with me. "Where?" she asked. "Could you look after us? In a strange place? With a thrall's brand on your cheek?"

'She told Teksla to say goodbye. When he hugged me, he was still clutching the broken bits of his little boat. Cailin kissed me and ran back into the darkness. She'll have gone by now with the man of the Ravens, but one day, I promise, I'll go back for Teksla.'

Wondering if it was the right thing to say, Bhòid spoke. 'My twin sister is the best thing in my life.' For the first time, Ruad really looked at him, understanding dawning in the depths of his blue eyes as Bhòid started his story.

16

ANGRY TOTEMS

CU GROWLED SOFTLY. Sulaire looked up from the roots she was easing from the muddy soil to see Parsa inching his way further up the burn. A she-bear had come out of the forest and was standing in a pool upstream above a set of rapids, ready to catch a salmon at the end of its leap. Sulaire wouldn't have worried about the bear herself—she was far enough away and had plenty of fish to eat—but her cub was rootling and snuffling in the rocks near her. It was the cub Parsa was intent on, pushing at the edge of a safe distance between him and the bear. Sulaire gave a piercing whistle and the boy turned towards her. She didn't know if it was a sixth sense that told him when she wanted him; or if Jak, fluttering at the boy's shoulder, had somehow transmitted her message; or if the whistle was one sound that could penetrate the silence in his head.

Come, she gestured vigorously, and with a last glance at the cub, Parsa came, contenting himself, for now, with picking burrs out of Cu's fur. The lower pool where Sulaire was working flowed in its turn into a second set of rapids and the air was full of the sound of running water and the hum of bees.

On the hill beyond, she could see the Hounds on their early-morning training run. The Deer-Hounds—boys and girls who had yet to reach their fifteenth summer—ran valiantly in the wake of the Boar-Hounds—the lads of fifteen summers who'd take manhood this year on the Day of Autumn Balance. If they acquitted themselves well in the Boar Hunt. If they survived.

As they skirted the hill towards the stream, yodelling like the hounds they were named for, the bear nudged her cub safely back into the forest. Leaping over the burn, the Hounds bounded down the steep side of the stream as if it were as steady under their feet as flat ground, and passed Sulaire and Parsa. Athru kept his eyes fixed straight ahead, as if he hadn't seen them, but Sulaire knew that he had. Not once since Midsummer, when she had told him about the salmon, had he looked at her, or spoken, or smiled. All the same, she'd noticed that at night, when the Hounds brought the Great Ones platters of fresh roast salmon and jars of ale, Athru was always carrying ale. She wondered what he was eating if he couldn't stomach salmon.

Late that afternoon, Sulaire came out of the healing hall, tired from the long battle she and Oran had had to ease a child backwards from his mother's womb. As she went down to the burn to wash the muck from her hands, she saw Athru standing under an alder, waiting. He stood there until she'd washed, and then he came towards her, putting out his hand to steady her up the slippery bank. His shoulders were broadening and he was lean and hard-muscled. Too lean, she thought, almost gaunt in the face.

'Sulaire,' he said, his green eyes troubled. He still held her hand and she felt a tremor in his fingers. He swallowed. 'I'm a coward,' he said. 'I've become a coward.'

She waited quietly.

'Each year I've run with the Deer-Hounds and watched the Boar-Hounds stand their ground with us behind them, watched them kill the boar and take their manhood. I was scared, holding the circle behind them in case the boar broke through, but I could do it. I dreamed that when the time came I'd be First Spear and earn my manhood with great courage.'

'And now?'

His grip on her hand tightened. 'The Hunt's a moon and a half away and already I'm afraid. Perhaps you were right, Sulaire. I keep dreaming of a salmon. He's angry with me.'

He looked so unhappy that she wanted to take him in her arms like a hurt child, but she stood there quietly as he went on. 'That day in spring … I ran from the bear. If you're right, then I've killed and eaten my own totem, and I ran away from Merak when I was wearing his mark.' He burst out, desperately, 'What happens to someone who serves the wrong totem and dishonours his own? I'm so afraid I can't think. Even if it's only a deer we're hunting.'

She looked at him steadily. 'Are you afraid of the boar, or afraid of your own fear?'

'Is there a difference?'

'Is it worse fearing that the boar might kill you, or dreading that you might run away and shame yourself?'

'Shame,' he groaned, his eyes pleading. 'Ask Oran to give you something so I'm not a coward.'

'There'll be a cost.'

'I have an otter pelt for her.'

'Oh, Athru,' Sulaire said, 'that's not what I meant. Prayers to the gods, potions for love or courage—it's not like giving someone tormentil for fever. There are dangers.'

'I'd rather die than be shamed.'

She sighed. 'Then I'll ask her.'

'Ask her about my totem,' he said. 'I must know, for certain.'

'Yarrow for courage,' said Oran, 'borage, mullein.' The old woman shook her head. 'He knows there may be a price?'

Sulaire laughed softly. 'He wanted to give you an otter pelt.'

'That would be most welcome,' said Oran, 'but you know what I'm asking?'

'Yes, of course I told him, but he fears shame more than death.'

'Then give him the herbs, a palmful every day in a tea. Three days before the Boar Hunt, double the amount. Is there something else, Sulaire?'

Sulaire hesitated. 'Oran, is it possible—could Kolnos have given him the wrong totem? When the bear appeared on the Day of the Totems, it had a live salmon in his mouth. Athru keeps dreaming of an angry salmon. He doesn't know what to do.'

The old woman looked troubled. 'That's something I have never known to happen. Add heather to the tea. It's good for clarity. Let him carry rowan to ward off evil. Let him ask Merak for a true sign.'

Next day, Sulaire gave Athru the tea and a spray of rowan leaves. All the days after, he came to her tent before dawn, when no one would see, drank his tea, and left with a quiet word. When she watched him from a distance, coursing with the Hounds in the morning, she saw how he pushed himself to be always at the front of the pack. When the Hounds gathered by the river to help clean the salmon the Hunters had speared, Athru avoided actually touching the fish by being always the first to shoulder the baskets of cleaned fish to carry up to the smoking fires.

He still wore Merak's token round his neck. It would be too hard, Sulaire thought, for him to take it off and face the questions, but when he came to her tent, there was a growing depth in his eyes. Sometimes his fingers brushed over the bear-claw as if he was ready to take it off. *The potion is working*, she thought, *but what is the price?*

Towards the end of summer, in the half-moon before the Boar Hunt, the wind shifted to the west and the rain came drifting across the meeting-place, day after day. On days when the sun shone, the air was damp and muggy, with thunder in the afternoons and drenching showers. Everything was mud. Mould grew on the walls of the healing hall.

A few days before the Boar Hunt, the weather cleared, the sun shone, and the trails began to dry out a little, though the burns gushed down the hills in dirty torrents. On the second dawn before the Hunt, Sulaire was outside her tent with Athru's tea, stronger, as Oran had told her. When she held the cup out to him, he placed his hands over hers, so that together they raised the cup to his mouth.

'Bitter,' he said, then gulped the rest down and dropped his hands.

She put the cup aside. 'Double strength this morning. Oran said. Then none tomorrow.'

He looked at her in the half light, fumbled at his neck, and shyly held out his hand. His bear-claw pendant, strung on a new red-dyed leather thong, lay on his palm.

'Not your totem sign,' she said, half angry, half afraid.

He shook his head. 'Salmon came to me again last night. I have prayed every morning when I drank the tea, and every night before I slept. Salmon is my totem. I have fished for salmon, killed and eaten my totem. Yet in my dream, I wasn't afraid. He isn't angry with me now. Salmon has given me his power. I can't wear Merak's token anymore. It's strong magic. It will protect you when I can't.'

As he bent to put the pendant round her neck, his lips brushed her cheek. When their eyes met, she saw the yearning in his.

'Not now,' she said, gently. 'I must find my brother first.'

'And if we find your brother?'

'I will find him,' she said, 'but beyond that I see nothing.' She took Athru's hand and felt the warmth flowing between their palms.

As Sulaire dropped Athru's hand she glanced towards the little tent and saw that Parsa had woken and was watching them solemnly. When Athru turned and smiled at him, the boy came close, holding out a cord knotted round a small lump of wood. When Athru bent to let the boy tie the cord round his neck, Sulaire recognised the little jackdaw that Athru had carved for Parsa. It was almost as if Parsa had understood everything.

Foraging upstream the next morning, Sulaire found a clump of the rare golden broom that was good for yellow dye and rheumatism. At once she thought of Ead. All summer she'd tried to keep out of Ead's way—aware of the Wise Woman's twisted jealousy whenever their paths crossed. She'd wished there was something she could do—a gift, a service of some kind—that might turn Ead's anger aside. Here was the broom. Ead was bent with rheumatism, using a stick even in summer, hardly able to leave her house in winter. Carefully, Sulaire started cutting a bunch of the yellow flowers.

It was only when Cu growled that Sulaire raised her head and saw that Parsa and Jak had gone. Starting to her feet, she saw them further up the stream, creeping towards the higher pool where the she-bear was fishing again. Her cub was bigger now, venturing further from his mother, downstream a little way, so that he and Parsa were drawing close to each other, too close. Sulaire whistled, but the boy either didn't or wouldn't hear.

Limping as fast as she could up the slope, she gripped Parsa's shoulder, shaking him with a scared fury she hadn't felt before. He looked up, frightened, but anger was hot in her throat, and she dug her fingers more firmly into his flesh, signing, 'No!' with all the force she could muster. Tears started in his eyes as she tugged him back down the stream to the clump of broom.

While Sulaire worked, Parsa crouched with his back to her, head down, sulking. Jak squatted beside him with ruffled feathers, but before long, Jak had hopped off to chase insects in the heather, and Parsa began investigating a water-vole's burrow.

Towards evening, Sulaire and Parsa made their way back down the stream. Parsa seemed to have forgotten her morning anger, and was running ahead, then rushing back to her, then running ahead again, tumbling and jumping about with Cu. Jak fluttered round them, none of the three watching where they were going.

Sulaire called Parsa urgently, but he couldn't hear her and she couldn't move fast enough to catch him. As they neared the meeting-place, Ead came round the side of a hut, and the dog and child cannoned into her, knocking her over.

As Sulaire bent to help Ead up, the bear claw pendant swung clear from the neck of her tunic. Ead froze, staring at it, and then, rising up to her full height, she spoke with a cold intensity that was worse than any shouting, 'You crippled thrall, how dare you wear Merak's token?'

Helplessly, Sulaire held out the bunch of golden broom, but Ead threw down the flowers and trampled them into the dirt where Parsa lay, too terrified to move. 'Get away from me, witch,' Ead spat, 'with your black spirit bird and your feeble-minded runt.'

Just then, the Hounds came running through the meeting-place. Athru left the pack and stepped between Ead and Sulaire, his green eyes calm and level. For a breath of time, Ead hesitated, but she was Wise Woman of the Beavers, servant of the Goddess, and Athru had flouted her in front of the other Hounds, who stood staring. Ead looked him in the eye, but, as he held her gaze, she dropped her eyes to his chest and the rough wooden bird hanging where the bear claw should have been. Her eyes sharpened with understanding.

'You have given Merak's token to the witch.' Her voice started to rise. 'You have dishonoured the Great Bear, your Clan, the whole Tribe. As servant of the Goddess, I curse you.' Her voice rose, higher and faster, the words losing their shape and meaning, a torrent rolling over the heads of Athru and Sulaire and Parsa, who still lay whimpering on the ground.

At last, Ead's curses stopped and she stood glaring at the small circle of watching Hounds. One of them hurried forward to pick up her stick, and she stalked away towards the council fire.

Athru shook himself, took Parsa on his shoulder, carried him down to the stream and washed the spit and tears from his face.

Sulaire followed slowly, plunging under the water, sinking and rising three times to wash away the curse. When they came dripping from the water, she was shuddering with cold, but Athru seemed strangely calm.

'Merak is more powerful than Ead,' he said. 'You wear his token. He will protect you.'

Sulaire shook her head, gripped with terror. 'Oran,' she begged. 'Something to ward off the curse. Come to Oran.'

17

HUNTER'S COURAGE

THE AIR WAS filled with a tangy smoke and the sound of Oran's chanting. She poured dark liquid into a cup, holding it to each of their lips in turn. As the bitter fluid slipped down Sulaire's throat, she felt a warmth round her heart. Parsa made a face, but as soon as he had drunk, the colour came back to his cheeks and the light to his eyes. As Oran held the cup for Athru, her other hand lingered on his shoulder.

That night Sulaire tried to keep murmuring the words of Oran's chant, but still Ead's curses echoed in her mind. Next morning, she woke Parsa and left the Gathering at first light, so there'd be no chance of meeting Ead. The sky was red—storms before nightfall—but for now it was dry as they clambered up the side of the rushing burn.

She headed back to the spot below the bear-pool so that she could gather what remained of the golden broom for Oran. And so that she might see the Hounds running past.

Near sunrise the Hounds came, and Sulaire stopped work to watch them running steadily up the slope. All day they'd be up in the higher reaches of the hills, scouting the tracks for traces of the boar, planning the path of the drive tomorrow, searching for the place where they'd bring the animal to bay. Just striplings, they ran naked except for their kilts, knives in their belts and throw-spears in their hands. Tomorrow, she thought, with a shudder, all they'd have to protect them from the boar's terrified rage would be their thrusting spears and the leather strapping round their loins. As they loped on through the early sunlight, Athru ran a little apart from the others. Sulaire saw a new grace and power in his running, like the curving leaps of a salmon swimming upstream.

When they'd gone out of her sight, she returned to gathering the dyer's broom. Today, the bear was nowhere to be seen and Parsa stayed close, unusually quiet, playing some complicated game with Jak. Near midday Sulaire took out her comb and picked the lice from Parsa's hair, braiding it into plaits like Athru wore. Stroking his bare shoulders—for the feel of him under her hands, for his living, breathing warmth—she started singing the song she'd sung sometimes to Bhòid when they were children, hoping that Parsa could feel some of the rhythm of it through her hands. After a while he slept, his head on Cu's flank. A gleam of sun glanced through the rifting clouds and fell on her back. She lay beside the boy, her arm round him so that she'd feel if he woke and moved. Listening to the water rushing down the burn, the woodland sounds of jay and yaffle, Sulaire could almost feel the curse lifting.

She woke to Cu's warning growl and sat up, staring around her. It was the she-bear and her cub, coming out of the wood to the upper pool. As the bear started fishing, Sulaire began plucking wolf-bane at the edge of the lower pool. Secure in the distance between them, she felt a kind of kinship with the mother bear—both at work in sight of each other, each of them keeping an eye on her cub. When Parsa woke, he saw the bears but made no move towards them. Instead he crouched near Sulaire, tossing sticks into the pool so that they floated over its rim and dashed down the rapids. Every now and then he lifted his head to look at the bears, but all the same, he stayed close to Sulaire.

Sometime later, she looked up to see the Hounds coming out of the forest above. They checked when they saw the bear, skirted the clearing where she stood fishing, and started down the burn.

At that moment, the bear-cub grew bolder. It clambered closer to the water, slipped on a rock, and fell into the pool. The water, rain-swollen, carried it into the main stream and down the rapids that tumbled into the lower pool.

Before Sulaire could reach him to pull him back, Parsa had leaped into the lower pool. The she-bear roared and came galloping down the edge of the burn towards them. Parsa grasped the cub and struggled to the edge of the pool, shoving the cub to safety, trying to heave himself up the bank.

The bear was closing in on them, enraged, heading for Parsa as if he'd attacked the cub. With a strength she didn't know she had, Sulaire snatched Parsa out of the water, flung him behind her, and fell, crashing down as the bear came, faster now over the rocks, almost close enough for her to feel its breath.

A shout, and Athru leaped out of nowhere to stand above Sulaire, holding his light hunting spear braced towards the charging bear. Her paw knocked the spear from his grasp and tore across his chest, flinging him into the lower rapids. The Hounds and their trainer came running, some driving off the bear and cub, others racing down the burn in search of Athru.

Grabbing Parsa's hand, her head hammering with terror, Sulaire stumbled and slithered down the slope to find the Hounds gathered in a circle round Athru's body. He lay half in, half out of the water, still and white. Claw marks scored across his pale breast, and his head lay on one arm, as it had on Sulaire's knee when she first healed him, with the same quiet look of a child sleeping. His other hand clutched his sheathed knife to his belly, as if he'd grasped it as he fell. The corners of his mouth were set in a slight smile, a look almost of triumph on his dead face.

Her vision blurred and her head spun. She thought she'd faint, but when she felt a tug at her hand, she clenched her teeth and forced her eyes to focus. Parsa was staring from her to Athru's body, where the little wooden bird still hung on the cord round his neck. A tear trickled down Parsa's face and she dropped to the ground beside him. As she held him tightly against her, she couldn't tell if the trembling between their two chests came from his body or hers.

The Hounds made a stretcher and carried Athru's body back to the meeting-place. Sulaire took Parsa's hand and followed. All she could think of was that Athru's arm was dangling and swinging as it had that first time when the Hunters were carrying him back to the Beaver village. This time too she wished she could walk fast enough to catch up and lay his arm more comfortably—as if it mattered now.

Long before Sulaire reached the meeting-place, she could hear Athru's mother keening. As she came nearer, she saw Fiada looking down at the body of his son where it lay before Mathan, Chieftain of the Bear Tribe. Ead was there, and Sagart, but thunder was growling in the piled clouds, the first drops of rain were falling, and, as Athru's body was lifted and carried into Mathan's house, no one had time for Sulaire.

She felt tired, so tired. Crawling into the tent

that Athru had made for her, she lay on the piled bracken. She was dimly aware of Parsa whimpering, touching her hand, and then moving away when she didn't respond. She hoped he had gone to Oran in the healing hall. Oran would see that he had something to eat and a dry place to sleep. All night she heard the thunder ringing and cracking in the hills, the rain tore at the skins of her scanty shelter and by dawn she was drenched.

A little after dawn, two of Mathan's thralls came to fetch her. The rain had stopped, but the meeting-place ran with mud. With the trails washed away there could be no Boar Hunt today, and the council fire had gone out. The Great Ones were gathered by the cold embers—Mathan, seated on his bench, Sagart the High Priestess and Ead, Fiada and the other Headmen. Oran too, holding Parsa's hand.

Sulaire saw Athru's body, lying before Mathan, covered with a cloak, and she knew that she'd been brought to answer for his death. As the thralls pushed her in front of Mathan, the Chieftain reached towards the bear-claw at her neck, and then drew back his hand as if afraid. Yet when he spoke, his voice was neither afraid nor angry, but stern and clear, a voice to carry to all who stood nearby. 'Why do you wear Merak's token?'

Sulaire bit her lip. She couldn't tell him about the Salmon. That story wasn't hers to tell. There was a long pause and then Mathan called for anyone who wished to speak. Sulaire stood silent while the storm of words broke over her head. Words had lost their meaning and all she could hear was tone—Mathan's questions, Ead's angry whine, Sagart's coldness, Fiada's voice—deep and steady, somehow not angry. At last, the words settled back into sentences.

'Merak is angry,' Ead was saying slowly, forcing her point home. 'Angry that she wears his token. Angry at us for allowing the cripple to come to his sacred Gathering. He has sent the storm to punish us. To prevent this year's sacred Boar Hunt. All along, I said the girl would bring ill luck on the Beaver Clan. Now she has caused ill luck to the whole Tribe and brought our Headman's son a worthless death at the hands of a she-bear.'

Looking down at Athru's body, Sulaire found her voice. 'See,' she said, bending forward and drawing back the cloak to show the marks of the she-bear's claws across Athru's chest—marks more powerful than the faint image of them that would have been tattooed on his chest at his Man-Making— 'see, Merak has taken Athru as his own.'

She saw Fiada start, looking from her to his son, understanding dawning on his face. Before he could say anything, Sagart, dark-faced and haughty, pointed her finger at Sulaire. 'This is blasphemy—that a crippled thrall should presume to tell us who Merak chooses.'

A murmur of assent ran round the gathered tribe, but Oran moved forward, raising her hand for silence. 'If Merak is angry on the girl's account,' she said drily, 'it's strange that he allowed both her and the child to escape from the she-bear.'

'Kill them both,' cried Ead, 'the child and the cripple! They have defiled our Gathering.'

At that Mathan stood up, his bear-skin draped round his shoulders. 'I am the Chieftain of the Bear Tribe. It is for me, and me alone, to speak the will of Merak. Rebuild the council fire.'

While thralls were bringing armfuls of the dry wood always stored beside Mathan's house, the Headmen knelt to build a small stone hearth amongst the ashes of the great council fire and pile up a bonfire of sticks and branches. One of the Headmen used his flint and strike-stone to kindle a torch, handing it to Mathan who plunged it into the waiting fire.

Wreathed in smoke, Mathan spoke again. 'Sagart, Moon Priestess, prepare the sacred drink.'

Almost reluctantly, Sagart took an aurochs horn from the acolyte who stood behind her, added a powder that hissed in the drink, and then passed the horn to Mathan. As he drank from it, very slowly, he seemed to shrink into himself, hunched and suddenly old. But when he threw the last drops into the sacred fire, flames shot up, green and blue and orange. Mathan roused himself and rose to his full height, his dark-grey hair sweeping back from his temples like an eagle's wings. One of the Headmen passed him his great staff of judgement, carved with sacred patterns.

Quiet but resonant, the old Chieftain's voice reached everyone waiting round the Council Fire. 'Merak has marked Athru as his own. We honour the youth's courage. We mourn the death of one so brave, so near to Manhood.' He paused, sighed, and spoke again. 'Those responsible for his death—the girl and the child Parsa—must bear the consequences. Ead has called for their death. Nonetheless, the boy saved the bear-cub. We cannot spill the blood of one who has saved a bear. Instead, he is exiled from the Tribe so that his bad luck may not harm it.'

Mathan turned to Sulaire and she shuddered at his piercing glance. If she was to die, what would happen to Parsa—exiled, five summers old, deaf, and alone? She raised her eyes, pleading. The old man returned her look, and in the exchange of vision, it seemed to her that each of them saw many things, that the old man was battling with the spirits on her account. He spoke, harshly, as if each word was dragged out of him, 'The young woman has brought harm ...' he faltered, then lifted his chin and went on, 'ill luck, harm, but also healing. She is exiled, so that the Tribe may cleanse itself from her ill luck. Tonight, after dark, they must be gone. They must travel by the lesser paths so that no one may know where they go. They are taboo. No one may speak to them or help them.'

'And the bear token?' cried Ead. 'That must be taken from her!'

'Peace, woman,' sighed Mathan as if he was infinitely tired. 'No one may take Merak's token away once it has been given.'

At a gesture from Mathan, his thralls took Sulaire and Parsa to their tent. Parsa flung himself down beside Cu and slept. For a long time, Sulaire crouched on the damp earth, stunned. All she could think of was that the Hounds would be carrying Athru up to the burying place and laying him in the earth and she could not go with them.

She grew parched with thirst, but there was no water in their pot. Drinking would have to wait until darkness. She started to work the lashings of their tent undone, but she was numb and clumsy and Athru had tied the knots too well.

As the evening sun slanted across the meeting-place, Oran walked purposefully towards them, carrying a pot. When Sulaire stared at her, the old woman shook her head. 'I do not believe in this taboo. Mathan did as a Chieftain must to keep the peace, but I don't believe this taboo is of the gods. No one will dare question me. No one will risk angering the Healer who might send them the bloody flux and a putrid tooth instead of healing. Here,' she went on gruffly, 'drink this.'

Sulaire lifted the pot to her lips. It was warm from the fire—there was bone-broth in it, herbs and honey, and she felt the heat of it in her chest. When she had drunk her share, she woke Parsa and gave him the rest.

Taking the empty pot, Oran embraced Sulaire briefly, and put her hand on Parsa's head in blessing. She took a small horn from her belt and thrust it into Sulaire's hand. 'Take a few drops in water,' she said, 'when you most have need of it. The Sun and the Moon and the Twin Stars on your path, Sulaire, until we meet again.' Then she was gone, walking openly across the meeting-place in the twilight.

With new strength in her fingers, Sulaire untied the knots of the tent and used the hides to bundle their belongings. Parsa watched her, confused and tearful. Without words, she couldn't explain what had happened, but when she signed, *Just us two, we must go,* he shouldered one of the bundles.

It was nearly full dark when they set out. With Jak on Parsa's shoulder and Cu following, they took the faint track that led towards the thickest part of the forest where no one would see the way they went. Just as they reached the first trees, a figure loomed out of the shadows and she recognised the tall shape of Fiada, his eyes glinting in the near-darkness. He coughed hoarsely as if the words were choking him. 'Athru died to protect you,' he said, placing something in her hand, something hard and narrow, wrapped in hide. 'He died brave. I can't ask more than that. Take his knife, Sulaire.' He held onto her hand, and as a current of feeling passed between them, it seemed to her almost as if he was imploring her help. 'Sulaire,' he said again, but before she could speak, he had stepped back into the darkness and was gone.

Tucking Athru's knife into her belt, Sulaire took Parsa's hand and they entered the dark forest together.

18

NORTH WIND

LEAVING RUAD ASLEEP in the small hut, Bhòid tucked Caraid under one arm and crept down to the Narrows. The rain had stopped and Seren and Speir stood clear in the sky before dawn. The Sunrise Shore was deserted and no boats were on the water, but Bhòid didn't expect them so soon. The Day of Balance was near. Tomorrow or the next day, two more at the most, and then the Beavers would be returning from the Gathering, Sulaire with them.

Everything was ready. Yesterday, stitched and caulked, the boat had run easily with the tide as he and Ruad paddled round the north of Eilean. Now it was safely hidden at the edge of the forest. There was nothing to do but wait, forage, patch the leaks in the hut, keep watch, plan what to do when the Beavers came, and wait. It would be easiest if the Beavers camped overnight near the Narrows. The boys could cross under cover of darkness. Sulaire would be expecting him. She'd hear his gannet cry and slip out to join them, and they'd be away, careful to leave no footprints on either shore to show which way they'd gone. No one would think of searching for them in the forbidding dark of the forest.

Now that the time was near, he couldn't bear to leave the shore. He spent all day in sight of the water, gathering shellfish and seaweed, carrying them up to the hut by way of the burn so as to leave no trace on the sand. Ruad stayed near the hut, adding moss to the roof, grubbing for roots, keeping out of sight of the water in case his height and his red hair made him easier to spot.

Late in the afternoon, waist-deep in Bhòid's Bay, Bhòid was wrenched alert by a sudden shivering of wind, a change in the sound of the waves, a cloud passing over the sun. Something was wrong. Something had happened to Sulaire. He looked wildly about him but the Sunrise Shore was deserted, the firth empty. There was nothing to see, nothing to hear. All the same, he knew something was wrong.

He stared down the firth at the dark clouds massing above the empty water and then he found himself running back up Narrows Burn towards the boat. As he reached the place, Ruad came down the burn, looking for him.

'What's the matter?' he asked.

'Sulaire's in trouble,' said Bhòid, tugging at one end of the boat.

'We can't set out now,' Ruad protested.

Bhòid pushed him aside. 'I must,' he grunted as he went on tugging. 'I must find her.'

Ruad grasped his arm. 'Bhòid. Stop. It will be dark soon. The tide's about to turn against us. There's a storm coming. We can't go now. We can't risk the boat.'

Half-sobbing, Bhòid let go of the boat.

'Are you afraid she's dead?'

'No,' Bhòid said. 'No, she's not dead. Afraid. In bad trouble. But not dead.' He steadied himself. 'You're right. We can't go now. Can't risk passing the Beavers in the night. We must be here when they pass.'

As he spoke, the storm broke, rain sheeting down out of the clouds and lightning crackling across the sky. Whatever Sulaire was facing, Bhòid thought miserably, a storm would make it worse. There was nothing to be done. If the spirits would speak more clearly, he might know what else to do, but with only a sense of dread to guide him, he must wait until the Beavers passed. Then he'd know if she was with them or not. And if she wasn't?

How would he know where to find her?

He couldn't bring himself to go far from the shore, so he spent the night huddled under the boat. In the morning, there was still no one on the water. All day he felt a kind of numb dread, but towards evening it sharpened. He felt breathless, choking, and then the feeling eased a little and he felt numb again and very cold. She wasn't dead. Cold and afraid, but not dead. He couldn't feel where she was, where she was going. There was nothing to do but wait.

Sulaire pushed her way through the undergrowth, Parsa clutching her hand. Her eyes stared into the darkness, but in the thick forest she could see nothing. Blackness pressed on her eyelids and wormed its way into her ears and through her blood until she could hear nothing but the lurching of her heart. Her hands trembled, and she squeezed Parsa's fingers more tightly. She mustn't weaken—she must keep up her courage for him. His fingers pressed hers in return, and he pushed her with his hip so that she moved a little sideways. He edged past her and let go of her hand. Panic surged in her throat. She could see nothing. She was alone in the blackness. Then she sensed the rustle of movement just in front of her, reached out to grasp his shoulder, and could feel that he was just settling Jak more firmly into the fold of his tunic. Parsa's hand reached back for hers, tugging, and she realised that he wasn't afraid in the forest. Perhaps his eyes had become sharper to make up for his deafness. Perhaps it was his kinship with the animals. Cu's wet nose nudged at her leg, and she followed Parsa deeper into the forest, Cu padding behind.

After a while, despite the darkness thick as ever, Sulaire felt the ground grow smoother under her feet, and knew that Parsa had found a hunting trail that led uphill. Above it, the forest canopy opened a little, and she could see a single star. She touched Parsa's face, drawing one finger down over his eyelid in a sign that they should sleep here. She couldn't risk undoing their packs in the darkness, so they simply burrowed into some ferns near the trail. Huddled against Parsa, with Cu lying over their feet, Sulaire fell into a blank sleep.

Waking stiff-limbed in the cold before dawn, she knew that they must set out quickly, warm themselves, and get further away from the Gathering before daylight came. All day they clambered up and over the hills and onto the further slope, looking down over the firth. They could see the Cormorant village nestled below them on the shore. There was fire down there and shelter, but although Parsa pointed and tugged at her hand, Sulaire shook her head. They must not go down. By now the Gathering would be breaking up, the clans returning to their own villages and the Cormorants would know of the taboo. She dared not even light a fire. Eating a little of their dried fish, Sulaire and Parsa rolled themselves in their tattered hides and slept in the lee of a gorse bush. All night her dreams were full of Athru's pale face.

Next morning, they set out southwards. She knew that Bhòid was somewhere to the north, on the island she'd passed in spring, but the safest way to get there was the long way round, keeping always to the shore, so for now they went south. They kept to the slopes until they saw the Beavers' canoes passing below. Then they came closer to the shore, where the going was a little easier.

Sulaire's bad leg was aching, the dull weight of Athru's death on her, a numbness dragging at her footsteps. By late afternoon she was limping heavily. *If I'd only seen where they laid him,* she thought. It made things worse that she hadn't seen him buried. She hadn't been able to place the customary rock on his grave to give him her blessing. Sometimes when her steps faltered, Cu thrust his muzzle into her hand and she felt the rasp of his tongue against her fingers, giving her the courage to go a little further.

All day Parsa plodded sturdily beside her and when Sulaire could go no further, she sank down in a sandy hollow near a stream while he foraged nearby, bringing back sea-beet, shellfish and wood. Sulaire started a fire with Athru's knife and the strike-stone Fiada had bundled with it. As they roasted mussels on the coals, Sulaire sat looking across the empty firth. Somewhere to the north-west, she knew, Bhòid would be looking for her. Now that she was outcast, how would he know where to look?

In the middle of the third day, Bhòid saw the Beavers' boats in the distance, paddling along the

Sunrise Shore. They travelled slowly against the north wind and when the tide also turned against them, they pulled into shore and camped just past the Narrows. Bhòid couldn't see Sulaire in the boats, but perhaps his eyes failed him at this distance.

All evening he fretted, forcing himself to stay in the shadow of the forest, straining his eyes and ears for any sign or sound of her. Something told him she wasn't there, but he must be sure.

Late that night, the boys muffled their paddles with hide and launched the boat. Caraid knew that Bhòid was hunting, and lay quietly in the bottom.

All night, they paddled up and down the shore, Bhòid giving the gannet cry.

There was no answer.

When dawn was perilously close, Bhòid looked over his shoulder at Ruad in the stern. 'Take the boat back to Eilean,' he mouthed. 'Load our stuff. Come and meet me when the Beavers are gone.'

He slipped over the side, laid his hand on Caraid's nose to tell her to stay with Ruad, pushed the boat off and watched it move away, yawing with only one paddler.

Crawling through the scrub above the shore, he skirted the Beaver's camp and lay up in some bushes on the further ridge where he could watch.

Next morning, with the north wind behind and a fitful sun gleaming through the clouds, Sulaire and Parsa made better progress, but when they turned west around Wide Cape, the wind blew across them hard enough to make them stagger sideways and sometimes miss their footing.

They rested at midday before turning north at the end of the Cape, down the Long Loch, the wind pitching into their faces. Their packs were light, but by mid-afternoon they were worn out by the constant wind, the days of fatigue, and the cold— too cold for early autumn—with a damp bite to it.

Looking at Parsa's pinched face, knowing she looked no better herself, Sulaire called a halt at the first overhang that gave some shelter from the north. Parsa would have gone foraging, but she shook her head. He was only five summers, he had cared for her last night, and he was almost spent. Gathering dry roots from under the edge of the overhang, she lit a small fire. She doled out a little of their salmon, a very little, since it must be kept for the worst times. They took a few drops of Oran's potion, wrapped themselves in their hides and tried to sleep, curled together with Cu and Jak nestled against Parsa's stomach. All night Sulaire held the boy but still she couldn't stop shivering until Cu wriggled out from under Parsa's arm and lay at her back, nuzzling into her neck.

'We must find Bhòid soon,' she murmured to the old dog.

At first light, Bhòid lay flat on his stomach in the scrub and watched the Beavers break camp in time to travel north with the tide. As they took to the boats, he could see Fiada's tall figure and Ead's squat one. He couldn't see Sulaire's distinctive walk among the older women and smaller children who travelled in the boats. With a sick emptiness in his stomach, he watched the Beavers paddle out of sight and then turned to look out at the way he must go. Yes, he could feel she was somewhere to the southeast, but how did that help, when the morning light swept so wide over the eastern hills before him?

'Could she have died?' Ruad asked when they met on the shore. 'People die.'

'I would've known. I would've felt her leaving.'

'What, then? Would they sell her to a man from another clan?'

'She'd never go with another clan. She knows I'll be coming for her.' Bhòid paused, waiting, as if he could touch her spirit on the wind, somewhere to the southeast as the raven flies, but with no straight path across the hills and lochs. 'They've left her behind. Perhaps ill, perhaps outcast. We must travel towards the Gathering.'

'Do you know the way?'

'From what the Beavers say, I know enough. Hug this shore and keep to the south. Leave the mouth of Long Loch to the left, round Wide Cape, turn north into the Holy Loch. We just follow the shore.'

Running easily with the tide and the north wind behind them, they reached the mouth of Long Loch in mid-afternoon. Bhòid looked across the loch to the shore on the other side. So near. They'd reach it soon with the last of the northerly tide behind them.

Then he realised—if Sulaire was coming this way, she'd be on foot, walking along the shore. They'd have to travel north, then south round the whole loch to be sure they didn't miss her.

Soon after they swung north, the southerly tide and the north wind joined against them. As soon as they found a little cove, they gave up the battle and pulled into shore.

'You wait here,' Bhòid said. 'Follow me when the tide turns north again tomorrow morning. If I can reach her tonight, I will.' He bundled food and hides and set off along the shore with Caraid.

Sulaire woke with her leg stiff and aching. Even moving a little way to wash her face in one of the small streams, she limped heavily. When she knelt to tie the knots around their packs, Parsa signed to her to lash their smaller bundle over Cu's neck. Then he gave Sulaire her stick and shouldered the bigger pack. She tried to stop him, but already he was tramping away from her, Jak fluttering above him. She followed as best she could—the gods knew there was little enough in the bundle, and perhaps Parsa would let her take it again when they paused at the next small cove.

It was rough going over shingled beaches and gorse headlands, and Sulaire's leg troubled her more and more. Before midday the rain started, and they sheltered under a sloping bank. When they'd rested for a while and the rain had eased, Sulaire roused Parsa. They must reach Bhòid. Whatever happened, she must get Parsa to safety. She forced herself to move faster, ignoring the pain in her leg.

In a little while, the mizzle had started again, the northerly wind driving it into their faces. Sulaire looked desperately for shelter, but by the time they found a shallow cave—hardly a cave, just a hollow scooped from the rock—they were damp all over. They crouched in the hollow, but gusts of rain drove in and even though Sulaire peeled the bark from some damp twigs and split them with Athru's knife to expose the dry wood inside, she couldn't get a fire going. When she doled out a tiny share of their remaining food, Parsa dashed outside to gather snails from a nearby stream.

They ate them raw. Without a fire and warm food, with the water dripping from the roof and seeping under their hides, sleep was slow to come. When Sulaire dozed uneasily, her dreams were full of bears.

Before dawn, Bhòid was awake and rolling up his pack. It was hard going along the shore of the

Loch—shingle, bog, gorse, and the north wind in his face. Worse for her. He pressed on as fast as he could. At mid-morning Ruad caught up with him, and they paddled close inshore, with the tide, but against the wind. Bhòid scanned the slopes beside and ahead, calling, his voice swept away by the wind. Near noon, they reached the head of Long Loch and turned south. Now, running with both tide and wind, they were travelling almost too fast. Bhòid searched the shore more anxiously than ever, bringing the boat to a halt every little while, yelling Sulaire's name until his voice was hoarse. By late-afternoon the clouds were massed dark above the hills. Fearing for the boat, they pulled into a small inlet just before the sky burst, with all the hammers of Perkwunos flashing and thundering round their heads.

As the rain pelted down, there was nothing for it but to huddle under the boat, thinking of her, a lame girl, out in this alone.

By the morning, the rain had stopped, and Sulaire and Parsa kept one eye on the roiling clouds, and the other looking for any shelter they could reach when the storm broke.

As the wind picked up and the clouds burst, they took refuge under the first overhang they saw. The wind howled and buffeted around their tiny shelter, and before evening everything was wet—their tunics and hides, and their remaining food. There was no hope of lighting a fire.

They ate the last of their nuts and salmon, drained the last drops from Oran's horn, and rolled themselves in their sodden hides.

Too exhausted to sleep, Sulaire lay under the hide, trying to find a way to ease her leg. The pain was constant now, throbbing and burning, and she knew she couldn't go much further. Beside her, Parsa whimpered in his sleep.

Huddled under the boat, Bhòid felt Sulaire's danger as a tightening of his throat until he could hardly breathe. When he couldn't bear it any longer, he crawled out from under the boat. 'Follow as soon as the wind and rain drop enough for you to paddle and see the shore,' he said to Ruad, and set off, ploughing through the damp sand.

Caraid whimpered and ran after Bhòid. He loped south through the rain, over the boggy spit of gorse and onto the next stretch of sandy shingle. When it was too dark to see, he and Caraid wriggled under a stony ledge that kept the worst of the rain off them and tried to sleep.

Sulaire woke at the sound of Parsa moaning. When she felt his skin, it was hot. His eyes stared dully at her. Stiff and sore, exhausted from lack of sleep, Sulaire forced herself to walk up the small burn that trickled over the rock, where she filled their small clay water pot.

She sponged Parsa's forehead and chest, but by mid-morning his teeth were chattering with fever, his skin was dry, his lips cracked, and Sulaire was afraid. She couldn't leave him, but without fire and better shelter he might die.

The rain had stopped, and the wind and a fitful sun were drying the rocks. If she could find anything dry enough to burn, she could start a fire, but everything was sodden—the gorse, the marram grass, the driftwood cast along the sea's edge. North along the shore, east into the hills, as far as she could see, there was no sign of life, no smoke, no help.

She crouched beside Parsa, and there was nothing she could do except stroke his hand. They would die here, both of them. She was almost too tired to care, but a fire would be a comfort as she waited. She grubbed under the roof of the overhang and tore out a handful of dry roots. Not enough to start a fire. But hair would burn, and hide. Cutting shanks of her hair that had dried in the wind, and a few strips from the edge of her tunic, she heaped everything together. Then she took the knife and stone and struck a spark into the small pile.

At dawn, Bhòid was on the move. Too anxious to eat, he drank from the streams as he pushed himself to cover the ground faster, faster. He climbed to the top of a ridge to see what lay ahead. Only the empty shore. Again he gave the gannet cry, and again there was no answer.

He trudged across the next beach and to the top of the next small spur, and then, in two flashes of time, first Caraid started running down the slope, and then Bhòid saw a wisp of smoke rising from the end of the cove.

All too soon the little fire was burning down. It gave no warmth. Crouched beside Parsa, Sulaire was chilled to the bone. She roused herself, and stepped outside the overhang, looking north, to the way they would have gone, if they'd had the strength, to where Bhòid would be waiting for her, and she would never reach.

The sandy shore was empty and her heart cried out, *Bhòid, why didn't you come in time?* There was no answer, only the wind on her cheek and oystercatchers piping up the firth. She turned to go back to Parsa. She mustn't leave him alone for long. And then, out of the corner of her eye, she saw something moving, and there, bounding down from the bank at the far end of the shore, was a wolf.

Reaching for her staff, she stood guard over Parsa. Then she saw that it was a very young wolf. Running behind it came a boy. With their scent born on the north wind, Cu started growling in his throat.

'Quiet, Cu,' she whispered, putting her hand on his head.

As the wolf came close, it dropped to the ground, crawled towards her, and lay quietly at her feet.

The boy was coming slowly along the sand, as if he hardly dared to believe what he saw. She held out her hands towards him. 'Bhòid,' she said.

19

THE CROSSING

BY EVENING, BHÒID and Ruad had pulled up the boat and upended it, shielding the overhang, and rigged up hides on spears as an extra roof. With a good fire going and a broth made from some of their dried meat, Parsa was already mending.

They rested for a day before setting out. It took them five days to work their way northwards, Cu and Caraid running along the shore while Bhòid and Ruad took Parsa and Jak and Sulaire in the boat. Heavy-laden, low in the water, they could only make progress when wind and tide were with them and the weather was dry. Almost at once the dogs were friends, and Parsa, remembering Bhòid, never left his side.

Watching Sulaire, Bhòid saw how pale she was, beyond tired, wrung out by whatever it was that had happened to her. Whenever he looked a question, she shook her head. 'Not yet,' she said, but sometimes she reached for his hand.

Ruad worked hard at everything, but said nothing beyond what was necessary, silent and remote, unsure he belonged.

When they reached the Narrows, the north wind was up again with a sudden drench of rain. Bhòid knew they wouldn't all be able to cross at once. Not with Caraid and Cu added to the already wallowing boat. Not with the north wind on the beam, pushing the boat back into the firth. Nor could they stay here, exposed to any Hunters from the Falcon Clan that might come down the shore. There was darker weather coming in from the west, and no dry wood for a fire.

'Take Parsa and the dogs first,' said Sulaire.

The boys looked at her miserably.

'I'll be all right. It's not far. Not for long. Quick, before the weather gets worse.'

Bhòid and Ruad stripped off their tunics, bundled them into the boat, and hefted Parsa and Cu amidships. Jak settled onto Parsa's shoulder, clinging tightly with his claws, but when Bhòid tried to lift Caraid in, she pulled back and sat at Sulaire's feet.

'Now,' cried Sulaire, and the two boys shoved off.

Even with only Parsa and Cu in the boat, the two boys struggled to paddle westward across the

Narrows with the wind buffeting them sideways. If the tide hadn't started to run in northwards, they mightn't have managed, but the changing tide pushed them into the calmer water of Bhòid's Bay and they pulled the boat ashore.

The rain was sheeting down, the wind was up and the light waning. Running, the boys took Parsa up to the hut, then raced back down to the shore.

By the time they got the boat back into the water, the tide was setting stronger northwards, the waves slopping over the stern, the wind driving contrary waves over the prow. With both of them paddling hard aslant the waves, they reached the shore, well above the Narrows now, and Bhòid leaped out, up to his chest in water, and pulled them closer in.

Sulaire was limping up the shore towards them. Running towards her, Bhòid took her on his back and carried her at a stumbling jog back to the boat.

Now it was almost dark, only a streak of clearing light in the west to show them the shape of the island. The north wind was stronger, churning up the tide that ran against it.

'Should we wait for morning?' Bhòid gasped. 'At least we'll be able to see.'

'No. Now,' said Sulaire. 'It will get worse, and Parsa is alone. Merak will protect us. He's stronger than Mor.'

Easing the leather thong over her head, she touched Athru's bear claw one last time to her forehead and flung it into the water, chanting in a tongue that Bhòid and Ruad had never heard before. Bhòid helped Sulaire into the boat, Caraid after her. He used his belt to leash Caraid, tying a loop in the leash for Sulaire to hold. Running the boat into the water as far and as hard as they could, the two boys shoved off and scrambled over the stern and prow.

At first it seemed they would never get across— with the wind lashing, the waves threatening to swamp them, the boys paddling desperately, and the island seeming as far away as ever, but Sulaire kept up her strange song until, in a sudden lull, they drew close enough almost to reach the shore.

With a final angry gesture, a bigger wave took the foundering boat side on and it started to roll over. Bhòid could see the shore in swimming distance—only a spear-throw away. Grasping

Sulaire by the hair with one hand and his paddle with the other, he flung himself out of the rolling boat, pulling her with him. Holding fast to her hair, he got one arm firmly round the paddle and pulled Sulaire closer, with Caraid swimming, terrified, beside her. When Sulaire had a firm hold of the paddle, Bhòid let go of her hair, reached his arm round her for Caraid's leash and held it tight against the other end of the paddle. They swam together, driving the paddle ahead of them. Looking over his shoulder, he caught a glimpse of Ruad clinging to the capsized boat, swept northwards on the tide.

Twice, Bhòid felt the shingle under his toes, only to be swept back by an outgoing wave. The third time, as if Mor had decided that he didn't want them after all, a larger wave hurled them further in. As it withdrew, Bhòid got his feet to the bottom and pushed them the last few yards into the shingle. It was only now, with Sulaire safely ashore, that fright swept over him, and he found his teeth chattering.

But Ruad was still out there, and Bhòid plunged off northwards into the wind. In almost total darkness, he was running by the feel of the shore under his feet, but when he reached the spit at the further end, the moon shone through a rift in the clouds and he could see Ruad clinging to the boat's stern, struggling to reach the shore before he was swept beyond Bhòid's Bay and into the Northern Channel.

Racing into the water, Bhòid threshed his way towards the boat. He lunged forward, but the waves were buffeting the boat sideways, and he couldn't catch hold of the gunwale. With a last desperate plunge he clutched at the trailing bow-rope and pulled. With Ruad hanging onto the stern, kicking, and Bhòid tugging at the rope, at last their feet touched the shingle, and the two boys dragged the boat towards the shore. It was waterlogged and heavy, and they were exhausted, but just as they were about to abandon the boat, they heard a shout and a yelp. Sulaire and Caraid were coming up the shore, and Sulaire waded into the water to help.

When the boat was safe above the tideline, the three of them suddenly found themselves in each other's arms, sobbing and laughing with relief while Caraid's tail lashed against their legs. 'Parsa,' said Sulaire, breaking away, 'We must find Parsa.'

In the patchy moonlight, the lie of the land looked different, and several times Bhòid had to cast about him for the best way. He held tightly to Sulaire's hand, ready to steady her every time she stumbled.

When they reached the hut, Parsa was shivering and whimpering with fright and Cu was trying to comfort him by licking his nose. Everything in the small shelter was sodden. When Bhòid built the hut, he'd made it big enough for himself and Caraid and Sulaire, but there was barely room for Ruad, Parsa, and a full-grown dog besides. It was far too cramped inside to light a fire, but there was food stored in the rafters and for the first time in many days they ate their fill. With just enough floor-space for them all to lie down, they were soon warm in the heat from each other's bodies, and the air grew fuggy with the smell of damp dog fur.

In the morning the weather cleared and they headed up Narrows Burn. They were all exhausted, and the deer-tracks were wet and slippery, water pouring in runnels from the hillside. In the worst places, the boys carried Sulaire and Parsa.

As they came over the crest of the last hill, the Glen opened before them, the setting sun sending shafts of gold over the grass and huts of the Baile.

The dogs broke into a run, Parsa trotting after them, and with a glance at the twins, Ruad followed Parsa.

Bhòid paused under the sycamore, hoping that Feorag would show herself to welcome Sulaire, but there was no sign of the squirrel. Watching Ruad and Parsa moving about the Baile, Bhòid felt suddenly shy, as he had when Ruad had been so scornful about what he'd built. It seemed so little to carry them all safe through the winter.

Sulaire looked slowly from the new house, the two huts, the burn and the gorse-brake to Bhòid and her eyes widened. 'You've built so much,' she said. 'You kept yourself alive and built all this and you found me in time.' Her face quivered, and, for the first time, she wept. Bhòid put his arms around her.

'Athru,' she sobbed. 'Athru.'

'Athru?' Bhòid murmured, catching himself back from questioning her grief.

'He's dead,' she wailed, and he felt her shuddering against him.

He held her firmly, waiting for her to tell him, and when her tears were spent and the story told, Bhòid looked at her, surprised to find a tear stealing down his own cheek.

'If you had healed him earlier,' he said, 'we might have been friends after all. Poor Athru.'

'Not poor,' she said firmly, 'brave and kind. In the end.'

'Because of you,' Bhòid said quietly. 'Without you, he couldn't … I couldn't.'

Above their heads, the squirrel's red tail flickered and the twins looked up together. 'Feorag is the spirit of fire,' Bhòid said. He felt his sister's hand in his as they bowed. 'Thank you,' he heard her say to the squirrel, and then she grinned at her brother with the old mischief in her eyes. 'It took you long enough to see it.' She dropped his hand and headed down the slope.

Bhòid followed as she ducked into the house where Ruad and Parsa had set the fire ready. She knelt by the hearth, took out Athru's knife and struck the strike-stone against its blade. Sparks fell into the lichen at the base of their hearth-fire, and Bhòid saw the glow between Sulaire's fingers as the first flames took hold.

THE END

HISTORICAL NOTES

This story is set in Argyll, Scotland in the late Mesolithic Age (ca. 4,500-6,500 BCE). The early chapters take place at the head of Glendaruel. Bhòid's *Eilean* is the Island of Bute *(Eilean Bhòid* in Gaelic) and the Gathering takes place along the River Eachaig at the head of Holy Loch.

Twin Stars follows the story of Bute's first permanent settler, Bhòid, and his sister Sulaire. It is not known exactly when Mesolithic people arrived on Bute, but the first visitors were probably itinerant foragers.

Although there has been a lot of research into Mesolithic climate, vegetation, animals and technology, archaeological evidence remains patchy. As these people lived in thatched houses rather than in caves, their artefacts have not survived as well as those of the earlier Palaeolithic cave-dwellers. Little is known of what they thought and believed, so the story of Bhòid's Clan is an imaginative reconstruction rather than a historical account.

As far as possible, I have checked the plausibility of the events, landscape and technologies I describe. The Prophet Elisha (c. 850 BCE) is credited with resuscitating a child by laying his mouth to the child's mouth (Kings II Chapter 4); cardio-pulmonary resuscitation is recorded in the Chinese 5th dynasty (2465–2325 BCE); some stories of the Egyptian Goddess Isis dating from c. 2350–c. 2100 BCE relate that she restored her husband Osiris to life with a kiss. As for the fever that cripples Sulaire, there is an ancient Egyptian wall-painting of a man with a leg withered by polio.

For the sake of the stories, I have allowed myself freedom with the pace of technological development on the island, imagining Ruad using a granite axe and Sulaire a flint knife rather than the Mesolithic microliths more commonly found on Bute. However, both axes and flint knives were invented in the Palaeolithic period, and by the time I have imagined Bhòid arriving on Bute, Neolithic technologies were already developing in eastern Europe, and trading routes between Britain and the mainland were well established.

Bhòid's home, the Baile, is set on the site of the abandoned township, Achavoulig Butt, near the top of Glen More, and any evidence of the tools he and his clan used may have been buried under later dwellings.

The latest research suggests that Bhòid's people had dark skin and hair and blue eyes, but I have also introduced some characters who may be forebears of Celts or Scandinavians, characters with red or fair hair.

Since these people left no written records, we do not know their names. I have chosen names from Proto-Indo-European, Scots and Irish-Gaelic words that say something about their characters or their story: while Bhòid's name comes from the Gaelic for 'Bute', Sulaire's name comes from the Gaelic for gannet, 'Sùlaire'.

TO BE CONTINUED IN

Water-stone
Volume II

LIST OF NAMES

Gods, Stars and Totems:

Perkwunos:	The Thunder God (Perkwunos, *Thunder*—Proto-Indo-European)
Ullr:	The God of the Hunt, the Constellation Orion (Ullr, Norse God of archery)
Merak:	The Great Bear (After the star Merak in the Constellation of the Great Bear)
Seren:	The Sister Sky Twin (Seren, *Star*—Welsh)
Speir:	The Brother Sky Twin (Spéir, *Sky*—Irish)
Feorag:	Bhòid's Squirrel Totem (Feòrag, *Squirrel*—Scots Gaelic)
Talamh:	The Earth Mother (Talamh, *Earth*—Scots Gaelic)
Mor:	The Sea God (Môr, *Sea*—Welsh)

Main Characters:

Bhòid:	Thrall boy of the Beaver Clan (Bhòid, *Name of Isle of Bute*—Scots Gaelic)

Sulaire:	Bhòid's twin sister (Sùlaire, *Gannet*—Scots Gaelic)
Athru:	Son of the Headman of the Beaver Clan (Athrú, *Change*—Irish)
Parsa:	Sulaire's deaf foster-son (Parsā, *Sparrow*—Proto-Indo-European)
Ruad:	Bhòid's blood-brother (Rúad, *Red-head*—Old Irish)

Other Characters:

Fiada:	Headman of the Beaver Clan (Fíada, *Lord*—Proto Indo-European)
Kolnos:	Trainer of Beaver Clan (Kolnos, *One-eyed*—Proto Indo-European)
Lufar:	Hunter-caste girl, training with the twins (Lúfar, *Agile*—Irish)
Medjom:	Thrall-caste girl (Medjom, *Acorn*—Proto Indo-European)
Cosanta:	Mother of Athru (Cosanta, *Protective*—Irish)
Ead:	Wise Woman of the Beaver Clan (Éad, *Jealous*—Irish)
Oran:	Healer of the Salmon Clan (Òran, *Song*—Scots Gaelic)

Traill:	Thrall-woman, mother of Parsa (Tràill, *Thrall*—Scots Gaelic)
Mathan:	Chieftain of the Bear Tribe (Mathan, *Bear*—Scots Gaelic)
Sagart:	Priestess of the Moon Goddess (Sagart, *Priestess*—Irish)
Awija:	Old woman who helps Ruad (Áwijā, *Grandmother*—Proto Indo-European)
Ingen:	Ruad's mother (Ingen, *Daughter*—Irish)
Gaoth:	Ruad's father (Gaoth, *Wind*—Irish)
Dubh:	Ruad's half-brother (Dubh, *Black*—Scots Gaelic)
Cailin:	Dubh's younger sister (Cailín, *Girl*—Irish)
Teksla:	Dubh's younger brother (Tekslā, *Axe*—Proto-Indo-European)

Dogs:

| Caraid: | Bhòid's adopted wolf (Caraid, *Friend*—Scots Gaelic) |
| Cu: | Parsa's dog (Cù, *Dog*—Scots Gaelic) |

Places:

The Beaver village:	The Clachan of Glendaruel
Eilean:	The island Bhòid flees to (Isle of Bute—Eilean Bhòid)
Bradan River:	(Bradan, *Salmon*—Scots Gaelic) Eachaig River, at the head of Holy Loch
Long Loch:	Loch Striven
The Baile:	Achavoulig Butt, Glen More, Isle of Bute

ACKNOWLEDGEMENTS

Many people have encouraged, supported and challenged me during the writing of this book. I am especially grateful to my whole family and to my wife Susan. Vickie Mackenzie was an invaluable source of local knowledge and sensitive editorial advice, and Liz Monument was both tough and generous in her mentoring: I have learned a great deal from both of them. Thanks also to David Brown from Wild Bute for advice on vegetation, and to mapmaker Ruth Slater for her patient artistry in developing the map; and to Karen Crombie for her clear-thinking proof-reading. I am deeply indebted to the expertise of the team at Indiemosh (Jenny Mosher, Astrid Stephens and Ally Mosher) who prepared the manuscript for publication; and to my sister Lucinda for the cover. Varuna the Writers House in Katoomba provided a haven of inspiration, contact with other writers, and dedicated writing time. Finally, my heartfelt thanks to all the staff and customers of the Little Teapot Café in Davistown who made me so many coffees and took such an interest in my progress.

ABOUT THE AUTHOR

Charlotte Clutterbuck has written many essays, stories and journal articles, four books of poems and *Encounter with God* (Ashgate). She also wrote the film scripts for the animated series *The Web* (ABC TV) which received several national and international awards.

Charlotte taught high school English, lectured on literature in the Clemente program at the Australian Catholic University, and led many workshops in grammar and creative writing at the NSW and Canberra Writers Centres. She has also lectured in Indigenous programs at Macquarie University, worked as an English teacher and editor, and advised PhD Students in the Business School at UNSW at the Australian Defence Force Academy.

Now living with her wife on an estuary on the NSW Central Coast, Charlotte spends a lot of time birdwatching, tending her vegetable garden, stargazing and taking her grandchildren kayaking.

Twin Stars is the first volume of The Gannet Quartet, a series of novels set in stone-age Scotland.

For more about Charlotte and her writing visit:
https://www.charlotteclutterbuck.com

Printed in Australia
Ingram Content Group Australia Pty Ltd
AUHW021659271023
385663AU00001B/1

9 781923 065093